"Is this wrong?" Olivia moaned and removed the spectacles from her face as soon as she and Stella were heading away from town.

Had she not been hiding behind them, she never could have gone through that fiasco of an interview.

"Wrong? For who? Dr. McCory advertised. He needs a temporary wife, his grandmother needs a companion, you need a job, and I need—" Stella grimaced, looking over at Olivia with a puppy dog expression in her eyes. "I needed. . . to stay out of things?"

Olivia burst into laughter, shaking her head. That helped release the tension she'd felt from the moment Dr. Neil McCory walked into that restaurant with a Bible. "It's a little late to stay out of things, don't you think?"

Stella laughed then, and having driven out of town, yanked off the brown wig and handed it to Olivia. She shook her head while the curls bounced back to life. "Well, we did it. You're on your way to being a married woman."

"Oh, don't say it that way. I'm on my way to a job."

"But," Stella emphasized, "the job is acting like a married woman."

"How do I do that?"

Stella glanced at her and grinned. "Just pretend you love. . . Neil."

YVONNE LEHMAN is an award-winning, bestselling author of forty-two books, including mainstream, mystery, romance, young adult, and women's fiction. Her recent books are *Carolina*, *South Carolina*, *Coffee Rings*, *Moving the Mountain*, and *By Love Acquitted*. Recent novellas are in the collections *Schoolhouse Brides* and *Carolina Carpenter Brides*. Founder and director of her own writers' conference for seventeen years, she now directs the Blue Ridge Mountains Christian Writers Conference held annually at the Ridgecrest/LifeWay Conference Center near Asheville, North Carolina.

Books by Yvonne Lehman

HEARTSONG PRESENTS

HP37—Drums of Shelomoh
HP82—Southern Gentleman
HP126—Mountain Man
HP201—A Whole New World
HP218—Hawaiian Heartbeat
HP290—After the Storm
HP305—Call of the Mountain
HP338—Somewhere a
      Rainbow

HP357—Whiter Than Snow
HP373—Catch of a Lifetime
HP402—Secret Ballot
HP440—The Stranger's Kiss
HP510—Past the Ps Please
HP533—On a Clear Day
HP703—Moving the Mountain
HP746—By Love Acquitted

A Bride Idea

Yvonne Lehman

Heartsong Presents

Dedicated to the members of my writers' group who patiently allow me to brainstorm with them and who offer their valuable opinions: Lori, Lisa, Michelle, Debbie, Phoebe, Ann, Aileen, Gloria, David, and Steven

KAREN LEE VAUGHN
1708 Beverly Dr.
Marion, IL 62959

A note from the Author:
I love to hear from my readers! You may correspond with me by writing:

Yvonne Lehman
Author Relations
PO Box 721
Uhrichsville, OH 44683

ISBN 978-1-59789-620-7

A BRIDE IDEA

All scripture quotations are taken from the King James Version of the Bible.

All of the characters and events in this book are fictitious. Any resemblance to actual persons, living or dead, or to actual events is purely coincidental.

Our mission is to publish and distribute inspirational products offering exceptional value and biblical encouragement to the masses.

PRINTED IN THE U.S.A.

one

West Virginia, 1916

WANTED: A bride of convenience for one year. A strong, young woman to marry an established man. Care for and be a companion to an incapacitated woman (no nursing experience necessary). The position requires some cooking and management of other employees. Respond by mail to DNMC, General Delivery, Post Office, Sunrise, West Virginia.

Olivia Easton never would have read such an advertisement in the Sunday *Sunrise Gazette* had she not been visiting her aunt, Stella Easton Kevay, in Canaan Valley. "Stella, look at this. It has to be a joke."

Her aunt's shoes pattered against the hardwood floor as she stepped gingerly from the stove to the kitchen table. She set her coffee cup down and looked over Olivia's shoulder.

Olivia tapped on the ad.

After reading for a moment, her aunt gasped. Then she read the entire ad aloud. Olivia watched her step back and plant her hands at the sides of her trim waist. "Well, I've seen some fantastic things in my travels as an actress, but this beats all." She shook her head of copper-colored curls, cut in the latest short style. "How desperate a man must be to advertise for a wife." She picked up her cup and walked around the table.

Olivia nodded. "And how ridiculous a woman would be to consider such a thing."

"True," Stella agreed. She sat across from Olivia on the long bench. "Here, let me see that again."

Olivia handed the paper across to her.

"Hmm," Stella mused. "The man can't be too stupid, using words like 'established,' 'incapacitated,' and 'respond.' If he wrote the ad, he must be educated."

"He may be educated, but he's got to be too old or ugly to get a wife."

"Maybe." A gleam of mischief appeared in her green eyes. "But ugly can be overlooked if he's rich. This does say he's established."

Olivia wrinkled her nose. "That means rich?"

"Well, it means he's not poor. He has a job or a business. He probably owns a restaurant or a hotel. Now that's an interesting thought."

"Maybe. But there's also an incapacitated woman." Olivia thought for a moment. "Incapacitated? But she doesn't need a nurse?"

Stella waved her hand. "Oh, he'd have a nurse for her since he's a man of means."

Olivia lifted a finger for emphasis. "*Ugly* man of means, remember. But why would he want a wife for one year? I know." Widening her eyes, she spoke in an ominous tone. "He marries a woman for a year, incapacitates her, and then seeks another."

Stella leaned over the table, speaking dramatically. "We have a killer here. Like Jack the Ripper or the ogre, Iago, in Shakespeare's *Othello*."

Olivia loved this silly game they were playing. As far back as she could remember, she'd admired her colorful, fun-loving aunt who was considered the outcast of the family. Her father's stories of Stella's escapades were supposed to dissuade her from wanting to pursue an acting career, but they only made Olivia more determined to be like her.

That's what got her in trouble with her father who finally said, "All right. Go spend time with your aunt this summer. See how different her life is than ours and ask yourself if you want to end up like her."

She'd been here for a month now. She saw how Stella lived and preferred her aunt's cozy cabin more than her father's rambling, lonely big house in the city. She'd rather be like her warmhearted aunt who encouraged her dreams instead of like her father who stifled them.

Olivia searched for more job opportunities. "There's an ad for a telephone operator and a nurse in Sunrise and factory workers in the city." She sighed, feeling defeat settling upon her. She'd hoped to find a job in Canaan Valley and live with Stella so she could save her money. Sunrise was ten miles up the mountain, too far for her to travel back and forth, especially since the roads would be too treacherous in winter months.

"There's nothing in Canaan Valley for me. I can't be a logger or become a blacksmith." Trying not to sound morbid, she added, "Too bad there's not an opening for a stagecoach driver."

That sparked Stella's interest. "Oh, but wouldn't that have been fun? Too bad stagecoaches aren't really used anymore. Being on the road is never dull."

"Oh, Stella. You're such fun."

Her aunt grew serious. "Your visiting with me these past weeks has been wonderful, Olivia. Much of my time is spent being alone, living with my good memories of the past."

"At least you have those. Since Mama died, I haven't had many good experiences to make good memories."

"You're young, dear. And your father is right in wanting you to be sure about your future."

"Father thinks I should find a man and make a home for him." She made a face to show her disdain of that idea.

Stella laughed. "You don't want that?"

"I don't want to live my life for a man. I want to live it for me. Isn't that what you did?"

"Yes, but Kev was an actor. We were on the road together. I would like for him to be here with me now that my acting days are over."

Olivia noticed the familiar melancholy look that came to her aunt's face whenever she talked about her husband who had died several years ago. Stella had truly loved George Kevay, or "Kev," as she always called him.

"Since Kev, I haven't met anyone I want to settle down with."

Olivia sighed. "Maybe I'm condemned to a life of tragedy as a spinster schoolmarm or a piano teacher and living with my father for the rest of my life. I just can't do that."

"Well, it looks like you're as stubborn as I am."

Olivia agreed. "That's what Father says."

Stella laughed lightly. "What he doesn't realize is that he's more stubborn than the two of us put together. But don't despair," she added in her optimistic way. "Tomorrow we'll hit the shops in town again. We'll even go to the logging companies."

❧

Olivia tried to be optimistic on Monday through Thursday mornings when she sat beside Stella in the wagon. The old gray mare pulled them along the dirt roads until they came to the gravel streets of the town and its stores. She loved spending time with Stella, walking down the streets and frequenting all the shops. But being told there were no job openings finally wilted her spirits.

By Friday morning, she'd given up. Barely touching her breakfast, she moaned, "Oh, Stella, I'm doomed to a dreary, lackluster life. I'll have to go back to Father and do exactly what he says. I finished college like he asked, but he refuses to pay one penny on my acting career. What am I going to do?"

Stella didn't make a quip this time but looked very serious. "It's not easy, Olivia, doing something your family doesn't approve of. And actresses don't have the greatest reputation, you know. There are hard times and heartaches."

Olivia nodded. "But isn't it that way with everyone? Father lost his wife. I lost my mother. I have friends who did what their parents demanded, and some are not happy. Oh, Stella, I want to be happy."

Stella put her arm around Olivia's shoulders. "Hon, the life of an actress isn't always fun, either. And sometimes a person has to laugh, even at herself, to keep from crying. But in being an actress, you can escape into the personality of another character. I love that. But you have to love it more than anything and know it's right for you."

"Oh, it is, Aunt Stella. I have to be an actress, or I'll never be happy. Father let me visit with you this summer to get the idea of acting out of my system. But it's in my system even more."

"It has to be your decision, Olivia. But you know you can stay with me as long as you like. You're a big girl now, and Herman needs to recognize that."

Olivia nodded. She didn't want to think badly of her father. "He means well. He really wants the best for me. Now that John and Sarah have married and moved to Wheeling, I'm sort of all he has." Her hand flew to her mouth. "Oh, I don't mean—"

"I know, dear. Herman has me as a sister but doesn't want me. He has such a stiff neck."

Olivia saw the sadness that appeared for a moment in Stella's eyes before she quickly recovered and smiled. "You owe your father respect, but you're not obligated to sacrifice your life for him."

Olivia felt torn. She'd lost her mother, and her stillborn sister, at an early age. She didn't want to lose her father, too. That would leave her only family as her brother, John, and his wife, Sarah. And she wasn't really close to them, either.

Despondency settled in, but Stella had the cure. "Did you forget? This afternoon you get to see me shine. Now let's make sure our duds are ready, and we'll go paint the town."

&

That afternoon, Olivia sat in the nickelodeon audience. Stella's exuberance at the piano, playing the background music for the movie, was more entertaining to Olivia than the action on the screen. Especially during the automobile chase scene.

"You were wonderful," Olivia said on the way home.

"Honey," Stella said, "this is nothing compared to the stages I've played on, where there are voices attached to the action."

"Oh, but the audience loved you. And all of them wanted your autograph."

"Three people wanted my autograph. But thanks just the same." Stella flicked the reins, and the mare trotted faster. "I'm more fortunate than most actresses in their forties, especially since movies are becoming more popular than the stage. I can't keep up with all the young actresses vying for the movie roles, much less for the roles on the stage. I'm afraid my days of 'kicking up my heels' are over."

"Humph. I've seen you wind up your phonograph and kick up your heels."

Stella laughed. "All right, so maybe I can, but the audience and the producers want young people. You need to know these things."

"I'm young," Olivia said. "And the stage would be okay. But I want to train to be a movie actress." She sighed. "All I need is a job."

Saturday's paper showed no promise. Olivia tried to count her blessings. At least she had this time with Stella.

Olivia liked sleeping late on Sunday morning and having a leisurely breakfast while reading the newspaper. "Oh, that ad is in here again from the man wanting a wife." Olivia sighed. "I guess that poor man just can't find one."

Stella laughed. "Not poor, remember. He's a man of means." When there was nothing fun going on, Stella made her own fun. "You know, we need to check out that man. Like you said, he may be a killer. It's up to you and me to catch him."

Eager to get her mind off her failure to find a job, Olivia joined in. "What could 'DNMC' mean? Does he have four names?"

"Oh no, it's some kind of code. Like. . .Dinner Nightly at My Castle."

"Or," Olivia said menacingly, "it may be a warning, like Do Not Marry Crazy. Remember, he's a murderer."

Stella nodded. "I'm not going to be satisfied until I find out what this is about."

"Are you—"

"Maybe I am crazy," she said, finishing Olivia's sentence. She laughed, as if "crazy" were a most desired state of mind. "This is too good to pass up."

Olivia's heart raced at the prospect of doing something so adventurous, maybe even dangerous. "We can't let somebody like that think we're serious."

"Of course not. We won't use your real name. And we'll put our address as General Delivery in Canaan Valley. We have to satisfy our curiosity, don't we?"

There was only one answer. "Yes, we do." She laughed with her aunt. "Now, what name will we use?"

Stella tapped her cheek, and her green eyes gleamed with mischief. "Well, for this Romeo, what else but. . .Juliet?"

two

On Tuesday, Dr. Neil McCory picked up a letter from General Delivery. He had received two letters the week before and had promptly torn them into small shreds and deposited them in the post office trash can. The letter writers eagerly accepted his invitation of marriage.

One, a not-so-young grandmother, vowed she was young inside, needed the job, had managed a household of thirteen children, and could cook anything over a fireplace, including possum.

The other came from a woman who told her story of loneliness for all of her thirty-five years, was strong since she had grown as large as her lumberjack brothers, and always prayed she'd someday be established. Except for having copied the word "established," her vocabulary indicated she hadn't had a day of schooling, and he could barely make out the scrawl.

He dreaded opening this letter. At least his address on the envelope was neatly printed. If only he could have found a solution other than advertising for a wife.

After a furtive glance around, he turned toward the trash can in the corner. Sighing, he tore open the envelope, took out the sheet of paper, and read the brief note.

> Dear DNMC:
> I am interested. Please send more information.
> Sincerely, Juliet Kevay
> General Delivery, Post Office
> Canaan Valley, West Virginia

At least this one had enough sense to question the sanity of the situation and want some clarification. He could appreciate that.

His slim ray of hope was immediately dispelled, however. Why in the world would any decent, respectable, halfway lucid female consider such an arrangement?

&

Olivia and Stella rode to the Canaan Valley post office on Wednesday, only to find they had received no mail. Afraid their fun was over, Olivia shook her head. "I knew that couldn't be serious. Somebody put that ad in the paper as a prank to see if any silly person would answer it."

"We only posted the letter on Monday. Give it time. Now let's prance down Main Street and go into every shop and pretend we might buy out the stores."

Olivia laughed. "Not being a woman of means, I can practice my acting."

Stella shook her head of curly red hair that Olivia admired so much. "Ah, my dear, you're my niece. And contrary to what some relatives might think, I've made some wise moves. After Kev was killed in that bar brawl, I had sense enough to begin saving for my old age. Not a lot, mind you, but I'm not destitute." She leaned over and whispered, "Don't tell ol' Stiff Neck."

On Thursday, Olivia stayed in the wagon while Stella went inside the post office. Soon Stella hurried out, her skirts bustling, waving the letter in the air. "It's from Sunrise."

"Open it," Olivia said. "I can't wait to see what a desperate man—or a killer—has to say."

"We must do this right," Stella said dramatically. "Let's sashay up to the restaurant."

Olivia hopped down from the wagon, hardly able to contain her excitement.

"This is better than any play I've acted in, Olivia. But we have a lot to figure out, so let's get a cup of coffee and mull this over."

They scurried along the sidewalk, drawing some questioning looks from passersby.

Stella asked for the corner table at the window. After the waitress brought their coffee, Stella used the handle of the coffee spoon to cut along the edge of the envelope. She took out the sheet of paper.

Olivia scooted her chair around to see it as Stella read the typed words.

Dear Miss Kevay:

Thank you for you interest. I will be glad to meet you at a place of your choosing for an interview.

Sincerely,
DNMC
General Delivery, Post Office
Sunrise, West Virginia

Olivia balked, dubious about the whole thing. "But of course we can't do that."

"Oh, you shouldn't have said that word," Stella wailed.

"What word?"

"*Can't,*" Stella said. "When anyone says, 'I can't'—" She broke off her sentence and began to laugh. So did Olivia. The whole thing was so hilarious. And Olivia knew that Stella had always been a daring person. She wasn't surprised when her aunt laid out a plan.

"Let's take the wagon and go up to Sunrise." She squeezed Olivia's hand. "Isn't *sunrise* a beautiful word? It's like. . .a new beginning. The start of a new day."

Stella's enthusiasm and optimism were winning. And if Olivia was going to be like her aunt, what better time to start? "Well, I guess it wouldn't hurt to look around."

"Exactly."

"But," Olivia cautioned after the bill was paid and they were hurrying toward the wagon, "you know I could never consider marrying anyone for a job."

Stella stopped and faced Olivia. "Of course not." Then she grinned. "But I could. And maybe this man of means would let you work there, too. And I'm sure, Olivia, you and I together could overcome that murderer."

The mountains seemed to echo with the sound of their laughter. But Olivia thought Stella might really consider this. She was in her forties but looked and acted young and was beautiful. She made anything seem possible.

On the ride up and around the mountains, Olivia marveled at the beauty of the lush green mountainsides forested with pine, sugar maple, oak, and spruce. One peak rose above another. Rhododendron, laurel, and wildflowers flanked the narrow dirt road.

"Look behind you," Stella said.

While Olivia looked, Stella explained. "Canaan Valley was once as lush and green as this. Now the lumber companies are stripping the land, cutting the trees. It's sad. But logging has become such a huge industry." She sighed. "That's called progress."

Olivia nodded. "Yes, like the tree trunks that are in the bigger cities with electric lines on them so we can light up our homes. It is nice being able to pull a chain or flip a switch and have light."

"Yes, it's not all bad. If it wasn't for some of those cut trees, I'd be in a pickle." She smiled over at Olivia. "Mom and Dad had a small sawmill on this land up here. When they died, your father inherited it. To his credit, he gave me a tract of land, but he kept the mill. I sold some of the land but still have my little cabin, and nobody's going to cut those trees around it."

Because Stella lived in it, Olivia could honestly say, "I like your cabin better than our house in Davidson."

Stella nodded. "So do I. That's something Herman can't understand. About me. . .or you."

By midmorning they came upon a sign: SUNRISE, WEST VIRGINIA, POP. 2,013.

"Let's drive around and see what this town offers," Stella said. They passed cleared areas and sawmills and railroad tracks and a black, smoking train, huffing and clanging around a mountain.

They rode past a church, a school, a hotel, and a hospital. After returning to Main Street, Stella led the horse and wagon to a livery stable where the mare could be watered and fed. Across the street was a lovely white, two-story house with a sign outside with the words LAUREL BLOSSOM BOARDINGHOUSE.

"Hmm." Stella expressed what Olivia was thinking. "Living and working there wouldn't be the worst of fates."

Olivia agreed. "The worst would be married to a maniac."

"Quite an astute observation," Stella said, as they began to walk along the sidewalk. "And of course we can't go inside the boardinghouse or the hotel in case I decide to apply for the job."

Olivia liked the charming town where ladies, gentlemen, and a few children walked along the sidewalks and entered shops. Several blocks revealed a saloon, shops, a restaurant, a grocery, a bank, an attorney's office, a medical clinic, and a post office. Farther down stood the depot.

"Years ago, when Kev and I were married, we came through here with an acting troupe."

Olivia detected a moment of sadness in Stella before her aunt whispered, "That's my future husband."

The man was tall and skinny, wearing a top hat and dark suit, and eighty years old if a day. He was an aristocratic-looking man, but Olivia had a hard time picturing him as Stella's husband.

"Or him." Olivia nodded toward a man on the other side of the street.

"Oh, you mean Humpty Dumpty?"

He did rather resemble a picture-book drawing Olivia had seen of a short, oval Humpty Dumpty.

Stella sighed. "The good-looking ones have women with them. Oh well, let's go into the Soda Shoppe and drown our sorrows with a Coke or a milkshake."

Olivia soon discovered her aunt had something in mind far removed from sorrows. "Here's what we should do in the name of common decency," she said. "In case our man of means is not filled with common decency, it's up to us to put a stop to it."

Olivia felt a nervous giggle coming on. Stella continued, "You can't go to acting school yet because you don't have the money. Herman would kill me if I paid your way." Her words were tinged with regret. "Besides, you have to want this enough to work for it. And you need to be able to give it up at any time without feeling obligated to anyone. You understand that?"

"I do."

"All right," Stella said. "Just in case this might be a job for you, here's the plan. Let's at least have an interview with this man with four names. Oh." She perked up. "The four names thing probably means he's either very wealthy or royalty and has 'de' or 'van' in his name. Now what were those initials?"

"DVMC? DMNC? Something like that."

Stella slapped the table with such force Olivia thought the straw might fly right out of the glass. "Aha! See? He could be either 'de' or 'van' or both."

"Yes." Olivia played along. "De Van of Many Corpses. I'll bet he's a mortician."

"We have to know. It is a job. And it's worth checking out."

In a matter of minutes, Stella had Olivia believing that man might have a good reason for wanting a temporary wife. "And you know I wouldn't let you get mixed up in anything objectionable."

Olivia knew that. But she also knew what one person considered objectionable, another considered perfectly reasonable.

Hadn't her own father called her unreasonable for wanting to be an actress?

But the possibility of just seeing the man was too big a temptation to resist. After all, Stella said she would do the interviewing as the "mother." Olivia wouldn't even have to speak to the man or let him know she was in any way connected with Stella. Ignoring the butterflies in her tummy, she marched alongside her aunt to the post office.

Stella asked if there were paper, pen, and an envelope available for her to respond to an ad in the paper. The middle-aged clerk, obviously taken with Stella's good looks and charm, gave her everything she asked for free of charge.

After writing the note, making sure she got the initials correct, Stella handed it to Olivia to read.

Dear DNMC,

Thank you for your note. Please meet me at the Canaan Valley Restaurant Saturday at 10:00 a.m. I would like to question you before allowing you to interview my daughter. Please bring a book with you so I might identify you.

Sincerely,
Juliet Kevay's Mother

Olivia swallowed hard. Maybe this was the answer to her dilemma. Although she didn't really believe that for one moment, she nodded.

Stella looked pleased, folded the letter, addressed the envelope, licked the gum on the stamp and made a face, then handed it to the smiling clerk.

Olivia had the feeling she had reached a point of no return.

three

Needing a break after a busy morning, Neil left the clinic and walked across the street and down the sidewalk to the post office.

There was a letter, again neatly printed. He almost smiled upon seeing that the letter was signed by the interested applicant's mother. He could appreciate a mother's caution. And he could appreciate a young woman who would confide in her mother about something this preposterous. He'd never let a daughter of his consider such a thing.

On second thought, one never knew what he might consider. Although he knew that mail-order brides had been an acceptable practice in some parts, Neil hadn't an inkling he would ever advertise for a wife—until now.

Nevertheless, despite self-reproach, anxiety, and a sense of helplessness, on Saturday morning at 10:00, he tied his horse, Sally, to the hitching post at the side of Canaan Valley Restaurant.

He'd already given himself every conceivable lecture. He willed himself to put one booted foot in front of another and go inside. As Mrs. Kevay had requested, he placed a book on the corner table at the front window and sat down.

The book he brought was the Bible, hoping that Mrs. Kevay's reaction to it would give him an indication about her and tell her something about him, too. He ordered a cup of coffee and, upon lifting it to his lips, marveled that his hand was steady in spite of his quavering insides. A man, especially a doctor, needed to be in control at all times. Even the worst operation hadn't affected him like this.

Three gentlemen were seated at a table near him. Snippets

of conversation sounded like a business discussion. Two fashionably dressed young ladies waltzed in and sat at a table beyond the gentlemen. He doubted those young ladies would need or want to apply for his job—unless they did it as a lark. That could be, since they were whispering and giggling.

Never before having been one to be self-conscious, he now thought he glowed like a bonfire. The sunshine streaming through the window made him uncomfortably warm. He preferred a dimly lit corner, but it was occupied by a young woman. She was staring at a magazine through spectacles. When her chin lifted as if she might look his way, he lowered his cup and his head.

His ears seemed to ring with the mingling of male voices and the young women speaking to the waitress. He was acutely aware of the distant rattle of dishes and muted voices from across the room. However, all other sounds faded away when he heard the turn of the door handle, the *swoosh* of the door opening, and the rustle of a woman's skirt approaching him.

Swallowing hard, he put his hands on the edge of the table and forced his gaze to travel up the dark blue dress and into the face of a woman. Thanks to instinct and having been taught good manners, he stood. "Mrs. Kevay?"

She extended a gloved hand. "Mr.?"

He briefly shook her hand. "M–McCory."

"Mummacory," she repeated.

"No, no." He hated this but rushed around to pull out the chair for her. "Just"—he forced himself not to stumble over his own name—"McCory."

She sat in the chair, looked up at him, and said without smiling, "Thank you."

Neil stared for a moment. What beautiful green eyes. He'd never seen eyes that color. He returned to his seat and folded his hands in front of him on the table. "The name is D–Dr. McCory."

"Dr. McCory."

Was she trying not to laugh? Some sense of reality returned when the waitress came over and he watched the interaction between her and the woman.

Mrs. Kevay's skin was exceptionally clear except for the dark circles beneath her eyes and a black mole on one cheek. Her navy blue dress was plain, and her dark brown hair was pulled back into a tight bun.

While waiting for the waitress to bring her coffee, Neil tried to act normal. "It's a nice day."

"Yes," the woman said. "The days are cooler now that fall is almost upon us." She removed her gloves, which revealed graceful-looking, long-fingered hands.

He stared, then looked up and saw that she stared at him. He sincerely thanked God that the waitress brought her coffee and refreshed his.

The woman dropped two lumps of sugar in the cup, picked up the spoon, and stirred. He opened his mouth to say some other inane words—he knew not what—when he suddenly caught his breath. It occurred to him that this woman might be the one applying for the job. He was in his early thirties. She could possibly be in her early forties. Yes, she could have a young daughter. But the only way to find out was to get on with the interview.

Just as he opened his mouth to speak, she patted the Bible. "I see you must be a man of. . .of the Holy Bible."

"Yes, ma'am." That helped. "Are you a woman of faith?"

"Oh." Her eyes closed for a moment. Then she looked back at him with a sweet expression. "Where would we all be without God?"

He nodded. "Exactly."

"Well," she said, "I am glad to hear that you are a man of the Holy Bible."

Neil felt that put a little perspective on the situation. He'd prayed that if this was not God's will, then nothing would come of it. He must simply lay on the line what the situation was and interview this woman, and daughter if she had one.

"Mrs. Kevay," he said. "I am a Christian. I have a medical practice in Sunrise. My grandmother owns the Sunrise Inn. This is difficult for me, and I would like to tell my story only once. Could I speak with you and your daughter together?"

The woman stared at the table thoughtfully. He felt sure she would confess that she was the job applicant. However, she looked over her shoulder and wiggled her finger at the girl in the corner.

The young woman hesitated so long, Neil wondered if Mrs. Kevay was trying to force her daughter into something against her will. That would not do.

Finally, the girl stood and began to walk toward them. He tried to size her up without being obvious. Describing her as "demure" would be an exaggeration. She looked rather prim with her hair in a bun at the back of her head. He couldn't get beyond taking in the wire-rimmed spectacles to see her face. Her high-necked, plain gray dress covered everything from her feet to her wrists. Just as she seemed not to have a face, she seemed not to have a figure.

Neil stood. The girl put her hand on the back of the chair, so he made no effort to step over and pull it out for her. The young woman did not look directly at him, nor did she smile, but quickly removed her gloved hand from his after a brief handshake.

Although he suspected this girl was not the one to help in this situation, perhaps he could help them in some way. They must be in dire circumstances.

At least, even if he could consider hiring her, he didn't need to be concerned—not that he was—about any attraction between this spectacled young woman and himself.

❧

Olivia sat, and upon seeing the Bible, she figured he must want to make a point of believing in God. She expected most everyone did, but she'd never had much experience with church life until the past few years when they'd moved to the city and her father insisted they go and hear a preacher occasionally, especially at Easter and Christmas or when he was meeting with a churchgoing businessman.

She had expected DNMC to be an undesirable man with whom Stella would converse and say this was not the position for her daughter. But Stella had given the nod, a signal that this might really be a job for Olivia. But how could any of them even consider the job of. . .marriage?

All right, she would act like the demure daughter of Stella Kevay. They could laugh—or cry—about this later. She had to admit that while sitting in the corner, she watched this man and thought him quite handsome. However, her vision was rather blurry since she had to look through the spectacles. Any man who advertised for a wife had to have something dire wrong with him.

"Would you like for me to bring your coffee over here?"

Olivia stared at the waitress as if she'd spoken a foreign language. DNMC and Stella seemed to be doing the same. Oh, they were all crazy as loons. Olivia shook her head. "No, I'm fine."

The waitress said, "I'll bring your bill over here."

Watching the waitress walk away, Olivia wondered what happened to the sense of fun she and Stella had when talking and planning this. This wasn't a game. She knew she would have to call upon her amateurish acting ability, and then some, to keep up the charade. She'd like to take the pins from her hair, shake it loose from that silly bun, and let this man see that she was not a woman desperate for a husband. There was more than one marriage-minded man in the city who had taken a liking to her.

"Miss Kevay," she heard but did not raise her gaze from the table. She dared not look at Stella, not knowing if she'd laugh, cry, or run. "I want to tell you and your mother," he said, "why I advertised for a wife. Then I would like to know why you would consider becoming my bride for a year."

Olivia had every reason not to look at him. She certainly was embarrassed at what she and Stella were doing. And how in the world would she answer his question as to why they answered the ad in the paper? She wouldn't have to pretend that she was speechless.

Maybe she could kick Stella without being seen and have Stella say she had fits or something that would make this man not want her as a wife. Not that she would ever even consider it.

They were all silent a moment longer until the waitress brought the bill for her coffee. She reached for it, but DNMC got it when her hand was only a fraction of an inch from his. They didn't touch, but she felt that if they had, she would have been shocked with an electric streak.

He laid the bill beside him, away from her. This man of means was going to pay for her coffee. Proving there was something wrong with him, he might even offer her a job. . . unless she did something even more drastic than look plain to prevent it.

four

"Much of this has to do with my grandmother," Neil began. He felt he needed to tell as much truth as he could without going into unnecessary details. A little family history might be in order.

"My only family," he said, "is my grandmother whose husband owned Sunrise's first sawmill. When the demand for lumber increased, my grandfather grew quite wealthy and built a big house in Sunrise. Their son. . ." Neil looked at Mrs. Kevay who seemed interested and at Miss Kevay who wasn't looking at him.

He continued. "Their son, who was my dad, married and brought his wife into my grandparents' home at their request. The men ran the sawmills, one for softwood and the other for hardwood. The women took care of the house and turned it into an inn since so many newcomers were settling in Sunrise and needed places to stay while looking for homes or building their cabins."

"I understand that," Mrs. Kevay said. "Here in Canaan Valley, the sawmills have about stripped the land of trees. Communities have sprung up overnight."

Neil nodded, but he needed to get to the situation at hand. "My mom and dad planned to have many children—girls to help run the inn. But I was their only child, and I became a doctor."

He wasn't one to disclose his personal life but felt some of it necessary. "My parents died in a flu epidemic when I was young. My grandfather was killed in a train wreck when I was in medical school. That brought me back to Sunrise to help my grandmother who had raised me."

Thinking that his once-vital grandmother was now an invalid wrenched his heart. "Now my grandmother has had a stroke, and she has a weak heart. The specialists don't expect her to live another year."

"I'm sorry." The soft words came from the young Miss Kevay.

Neil was taken aback by her sympathetic tone of voice. He looked at her and was immediately again struck by the sight of those spectacles that partially hid her face. How in the world did she keep them on her small nose? But what struck him even more was that he knew she cared. Anyone who took this job would have to care, not about him, but about his grandmother.

"Your ad said she's incapacitated," Mrs. Kevay said.

"Not entirely, but I didn't want to go into detail for the ad. My clinic and the hospital are near the inn. I live in the inn and could get a nurse at a moment's notice. But I do want someone to take her food to her when she doesn't feel like getting up. Someone to make sure she takes her medications and to do personal things for her, such as ensure she's all right in her bath."

Neil waved away the waitress who neared with the coffee-pot. This was no time for refills. Neither he nor Mrs. Kevay had touched his or her cup after the conversation began. He lowered his voice to make sure no one away from the table could hear. Mrs. Kevay leaned slightly toward him. "She's known as Mama McCory," he said. "Her dream is to see me married, which she feels will ensure that the home they turned into an inn will continue to serve the people and tourists of Sunrise."

"That's a worthy goal," Mrs. Kevay said.

Apparently he hadn't alienated her, but he couldn't tell about the daughter. He really didn't care to look at the younger woman and think about a stranger becoming his wife. She was probably thinking something similar. But he'd gone this far, and they hadn't left the table. "Mama McCory knows I don't have time to supervise the running of the inn."

"Why, Dr. McCory, can't you hire someone for that?"

"Hired help comes and goes. A couple who has been with us for years wants to retire. My grandmother needs a companion—someone to make her last days pleasant and give her a hope for the future of her family and home. You see, to make her happy, I need a wife to keep the name of McCory and the inn alive. I want to give my grandmother her dying wish since she cared for me most of my life and paid for my medical school training."

He felt it time to get to the point. "I need someone to pretend to be my wife for a year, be a companion for my grandmother, live in the inn, learn to manage it, be paid a weekly salary, be content with a marriage of convenience, and agree to an annulment after a year."

Having finished, he knew if something like this ever got out, he'd be finished in more ways than one and be the laughing-stock of the county. He leaned back, just then realizing he had been sitting quite straight and stiffly. He spread his hands. "That's my story."

Mrs. Kevay's eyebrows lifted. "Why, Dr. McCory, I would think a respectable, nice-looking, established man like you could find several decent women who would jump at the chance to marry you."

Neil wasn't sure if that was a compliment or condemnation, so he didn't thank her. But he did feel he needed to defend himself, lest they think he was totally undesirable. "Well, there have been a few who might have married me, had I asked. But I didn't care to make a permanent commitment with any of them."

"Ohh." Mrs. Kevay clicked her tongue, and he detected a gleam in her eyes. "You're one of those confirmed bachelors? Why, Dr. McCory, why ever so, might I ask?"

He might as well spill the whole pot of beans. These two

now knew more about him than he liked to admit to himself. "I came close to marriage once, Mrs. Kevay. But my intended decided that living in a mountain town was not for her. She was a city girl and could never adjust to my backwoods way of life." He felt the sting of that. "We parted amicably."

"Oh, that must have hurt your heart, having to choose between your grandmother and your fiancée."

Neil felt quite warm from the sun beating through the window against the back of his vest. He felt it all the way through his white shirt. For a long moment, he pondered her statement. In reality, he hadn't thought of it as a choice between the two women. He'd simply known a wife of his must love his grandmother and be a part of life in Sunrise. Now he felt like the sun was shining on his face instead of on his back and head. "Well, just as my fiancée wasn't ready for life in a mountain town, I wasn't prepared for a life as a city doctor. As long as she is alive, I will take care of my grandmother."

"But after Mama McCory. . ."

The sympathetic expression on Mrs. Kevay's face and in her voice led Neil to nod. "Who knows?" he said, not wanting to think of facing life without his beloved grandmother. He liked the way Mrs. Kevay had said his grandmother's name. "I want to make her happy as long as I can."

Mrs. Kevay nodded. "Dr. McCory, would none of those young women you mentioned consider this arrangement?"

He shook his head. He knew his face had to be red. "No, ma'am. They wouldn't consider a—" He stopped his words. Men didn't discuss some things with ladies. "They wouldn't consider what I stipulated in the newspaper ad."

"Oh, I see." Her voice had become singsong. "Well. This is quite. . .interesting, to say the least."

He cleared his throat and dared a glance at the young woman behind the glasses. "Miss Kevay," he said gently, lest he frighten such a passive creature—or was she embarrassed? "Will you tell me why you would consider this arrangement?

And something about your background?"

The poor girl closed her eyes for a long moment, then barely opened them but did not look at him or her mother. Was she deaf, dumb. . .or both? Or. . .something worse? Like. . . deranged?

He wouldn't be surprised if she had a fit. He felt like having one himself.

૨**ક**

With eyelids at half-mast, Olivia slid a sideways glance at the man Stella called "Dr. McCory." What kind of doctor was he? An animal doctor or a people doctor? She couldn't very well ask if he had a pill that might make her disappear. What had she and Stella gotten themselves into?

Strangely, she had begun to think of this interview as real. His story about the loss of his parents and his love for his grandmother touched her heart. She wouldn't mind having a sweet old grandmother. Actually, she'd begun to wish she might have applied for the job legitimately.

But she hadn't. She thought of her father's having said that acting was the worst kind of job for a decent woman. Wouldn't he squirm to know about this! Well, he'd made her squirm enough times. She took a deep breath, wondering what to say, and shot a helpless glance at her aunt.

Stella patted Olivia's arm. "Dr. McCory, it's difficult for my daughter to talk about her papa, whose livelihood comes from the mining town beyond Sunrise."

Olivia wondered what her aunt might say. She'd better listen carefully in case it became her new identity.

"Juliet and I live in a little cabin here in Canaan Valley. Before that," she said, "Juliet's life was difficult living in the mining area beyond Sunrise."

He spoke quietly. "Yes, I know something of the difficult life in mining towns."

Unexpectedly, Olivia felt the pain of having lost her mother. How could she say that her father was a wealthy man who owned several mines and logging companies? When she was growing up, they lived in a big house away from the mines— quite a contrast to the little box houses in which miners lived. After her mother died in childbirth, she and her father moved to the city.

Stella was painting a true picture of her wanting to leave the mining area. But she knew this doctor assumed she had led a life of poverty and misery. She hadn't lived a life of poverty—only misery.

But it was too late to tell the truth. This man had revealed his heart to her and Stella. That couldn't have been easy, especially since they were strangers.

If she considered this job, she never wanted him to know that she and Stella had begun this as a joke, a fun adventure. This man would not think it funny.

She decided to speak lest he think her not qualified for the position. "Dr. McCory," she said, still not meeting his eyes, "I did get a college education in Davidson, and contrary to what your fiancée preferred, I don't want to live in the city." That was certainly true. She wanted to be in New York long enough to attend acting school. Then she wanted to be an actress traveling the United States, maybe even the world.

"And you asked why I would consider this job. Only one reason, sir." She stared at the table. "The reason is money."

five

The young woman's articulate way of speaking surprised Neil. She obviously knew how to be quiet and let her mother talk, but he felt she had no problem providing information. Her words were few, but she had expressed them well.

Was there a possibility this might work? Of course this one meeting wasn't enough for any of them to make a commitment about the job offer. "If you are seriously considering this," he said, looking from one who met his gaze to the other who didn't, "I want to invite you to visit the inn and meet my grandmother. If either of us decided against the arrangement, I can say you were applying for a job. However, if all goes well, I can then surprise her by announcing my. . .um. . .our. . . engagement."

He wouldn't blame them if they backed out. Their feet might be as cold as his about this situation, so he quickly added, "After you come to the inn, if you don't want the position, then I will simply go on with my life as usual."

Mrs. Kevay gave a brief nod. Her daughter said, "Thank you. I would like to see the inn. . .and your grandmother."

"Miss Kevay, we will need to be on a first-name basis when you come to the inn." He took her silence as assent. Remembering the name on the first letter, he said, "I should address you as Juliet, right?"

When she nodded, he tried to lighten his mood. "I'm often called Dr. McCory, Doc, or Mac. But I think you would prefer calling me Neil."

Neither of the women laughed, but Juliet nodded.

If pigs sweat, he'd be sweating like one. Heat rose to his face again at what he must say. He dared not look at Juliet but

31

kept his focus on Mrs. Kevay. "There is the matter of dress. I will be glad to provide the cost of clothing. I. . ."

His voice trailed off when Mrs. Kevay's eyebrows lifted and her eyes widened. "You mean," she said, "you want someone who looks like a citified fiancée?"

He hedged. "Not exactly." But his grandmother would never believe he fell in love with this plain creature with grotesque spectacles, even if she did have a nice way of speaking.

"Well," Mrs. Kevay huffed, and he thought he'd completely alienated the two women. Her stiff manner now reminded him of a stern schoolteacher who had looked down her nose at him when he was a boy and scared the wits out of him.

"Just because we live in a small cabin in Canaan Valley and have spent part of our lives around the poverty of the mining area, Dr. McCory. . ."

He was already nodding, bracing himself for a cup of coffee being slung into his face, the thump of the Bible smacking him on his head, or a tongue-lashing.

The woman stared. She did have striking, unusual green eyes. They were extremely large. He swallowed hard. She drew herself up, and her upper lip seemed to curl slightly. Juliet, or maybe he should revert to thinking of her as Miss Kevay, appeared to inch back from the table.

"Dr. McCory, we will not take one penny of your money without giving one minute's work. We are honorable people, sir. And I have been in a city or two in my life and have observed young women and their clothing. You can believe I know how to fix up my daughter in the proper uniform for the job for which she is applying."

The younger woman seemed to become strangled on something, but she hadn't even a glass of water. Probably, like he, she felt about ready to choke on this entire situation. "About a uniform," he said. "I wouldn't want her to look like a waitress, although I do need someone who can cook or can learn."

Mrs. Kevay reached over and patted his hand. The length and curve of her fingernails surprised him, as did the softness of her hand. He would expect her to have the rough hands of a hard worker. But of course, there were many kinds of hard work. He put in more time as a doctor than many men he knew, but that didn't give him the calloused hands of a miner or a logger.

"Dr. McCory," she said sweetly, "my use of the word 'uniform' was just a figure of speech. I understand you want someone attractive enough that your grandmother, and your acquaintances, would believe you'd fall in love with her. And at the same time, she must be a sweet, kindhearted girl who doesn't want the fancy trappings of city life but would capture your heart with her goodness." She patted the Bible.

Neil felt a sense of fear and trembling that God might not be in on this. For what seemed like the umpteenth time, he cleared his throat. Mrs. Kevay was an astute woman—more so than he would have thought upon first look. But then, she did have those fancy fingernails. He'd like to have a look at Juliet's fingernails, but he surmised from the movement of her arms that she might be twisting her hands beneath the table.

"I don't mean to be insulting." He turned his head toward Juliet, and she as quickly turned hers away from him. "And this is not only about looks. It's about meeting the proper requirements for a job."

"I quite understand, Dr. McCory. The work presents no problem. And I think my Juliet can meet with your approval after I fix her up. And, too," she said with acuity, "I realize your grandmother would need to approve your choice. But there are two sides to this. I and my daughter will need to be certain that she will be happy and treated well in this position." She added very quietly, "If she is interested in you as an employer."

At that, Mrs. Kevay slapped her hand on Juliet's coffee receipt and slid it toward herself. He did not insist upon paying, since this woman's act displayed principles. Juliet ducked her head and had to push her glasses up to keep them from falling off her face. He wished they had. However, he said, "Very well. When would be a convenient time for you to visit the inn?"

Mrs. Kevay began pulling on her gloves. "This afternoon," she said and stood.

"Fine. If you will meet me at my clinic, I will escort Juliet to the inn from there."

After finalizing the plans, Mrs. Kevay said, "We will be there, Dr. McCory." She paid her bill and led her daughter out.

ea

"Is this wrong?" Olivia moaned and removed the spectacles from her face as soon as she and Stella were heading away from town. Had she not been hiding behind them, she never could have gone through that fiasco of an interview.

"Wrong? For who? Dr. McCory advertised. He needs a temporary wife, his grandmother needs a companion, you need a job, and I need—" Stella grimaced, looking over at Olivia with a puppy dog expression in her eyes. "I needed. . .to stay out of things?"

Olivia burst into laughter, shaking her head. That helped release the tension she'd felt from the moment Dr. Neil McCory walked into that restaurant with a Bible. "It's a little late to stay out of things, don't you think?"

Stella laughed then, and having driven out of town, yanked off the brown wig and handed it to Olivia. She shook her head while the curls bounced back to life. "Well, we did it. You're on your way to being a married woman."

"Oh, don't say it that way. I'm on my way to a job."

"But," Stella emphasized, "the job is acting like a married woman."

"How do I do that?"

Stella glanced at her and grinned. "Just pretend you love. . . Neil."

"Love?" Olivia shrieked. "I've never been in love in my life."

"Oh yes, you have," Stella contradicted. "Remember Coco?"

"My dog?"

Stella nodded. "You loved him. He had shiny, dark brown hair, and you wanted to name him Hot Chocolate, but your mama talked you into calling him Coco for short."

"Yes, Coco was my best friend and confidant."

Stella reached over and patted Olivia's arm. "There you have it. That look on your face right now is precious. When you look at Neil in front of other people, just pretend he's Coco and treat him like he's your dog."

Olivia huffed. "I'm not about to look for fleas and ticks on any man!"

They could still laugh and joke, but it was becoming too real and too personal. "Maybe we should forget this whole thing."

"Fine," Stella said. "You want to go back to Daddy?"

Olivia felt caught between a rock and a hard place. "Oh, Stella."

"Just call me Mama."

Olivia moaned.

After they returned to the cabin, Stella stood in front of her and held Olivia's hands. "Honey, if you don't want to do this, then it's all right. We'll look for something else."

"It's not that," Olivia admitted. "Now I kind of wish I had applied for the job legitimately. I don't like this deception."

"Don't think of it as deception, Olivia. Think of it as pretending—acting. Even if Neil McCory knew we responded to that ad as a lark, the two of you would still be pretending to be married and pretending in front of his grandmother."

That was true. "But what if something happens and I don't want to be committed to being there for a year?"

Stella smiled. "No problem. You can walk away at any time."

"But we'll be legally married."

"Only if you marry him under the name of Olivia Easton. But to him, my dear, your name is Juliet Kevay. The marriage will not be legal. You can walk away at any time. Now," she said, letting go of Olivia's hands, "let's get you ready to take a job of being an engaged woman, pretty enough to become Mrs. Dr. Neil McCory."

six

Mrs. Kevay certainly wasted no time. Neil told himself he mustn't either. After having sat in that hot seat all morning while the sun rose higher, he'd have to bathe and be ready to convince his grandmother that he was either considering hiring a maid or that he had become an engaged man.

After riding Sally up the mountain, he made a quick stop at the clinic. "Carter, everything all right?" he asked his young assistant when Carter looked up from the desk in his office.

"Couldn't be better," Carter said with a smile. "Other than taking a look at the stitches in Billy Hooten's hand, it's been a slow day."

"Great," Neil said with a force that caused Carter to give him a questioning look. "I mean, I'll be tied up the rest of the day."

Carter shrugged. "This is Saturday, you know. My day for doctoring. Like you always say, 'Don't call on me unless there's a dire emergency.'"

Neil nodded. "A couple of women are to meet me here later today. Just wanted to let you know." He left the office and walked back through the waiting room and outside to unhitch Sally. There was a "dire emergency," and this doctor wasn't sure what to prescribe for it. But he had to quit questioning this. When he picked up Miss Kevay at the clinic, where Mrs. Kevay would bring her—fixed up—he could change his mind before anything became legal.

Yes, that made sense, even if nothing else had since he'd put that ad in the paper. Upon arriving at the inn, he rode Sally out back along the cobblestone path and to the stable where Bart was tending the horses. "Hey, Bart," Neil said. "I'm going to need the buggy in a couple hours. Can you make sure it's ready? And see that Sally is hitched to it."

"You don't mean the doctor's buggy?"

"No," Neil said. "This is something personal."

"How personal?" Bart said with a gleam in his eye.

Bart had worked for Neil's grandfather and his dad and had been a pretty good substitute after they'd died. "You'll know soon enough. Just practice being on your best behavior."

"I'm always on my best behavior." As Neil walked away, Bart called, "But I can't say the same for Hedda."

Neil could agree with that. Not openly, however, and as soon as he entered the kitchen from the back door, gray-haired Hedda began her interrogation. "Where've you been all day?"

"Where am I most of the time?"

She put her hands on her ample hips. "Out doctoring, even on your days off. That's all you do. You had anything to eat since that biscuit you swiped this morning?"

"Not a thing. Are there any left?"

"None of my biscuits are ever left," she said proudly. She went to the cupboard, took a tea towel off a basket, and handed him a muffin. "Blueberry," she said. "You want coffee?"

"Maybe after I've cleaned up. I suppose Grandmother is resting." She usually did after lunch.

"Yes, she was outside this morning. But she didn't stay out long. She's just not herself anymore."

"I know," he said. Since her stroke, she seemed to have given up on life. "Hedda, if she's not awake before I leave, would you tell her I might be bringing a guest home this afternoon?"

"A guest?"

"Hedda, it's not certain. But I'd appreciate it if you'd make tea, then serve it in the parlor. Oh, and include some of those little cookies."

She was nodding with a sly grin on her face. "I'll be here. I wouldn't miss it."

Neil mentally reprimanded himself for feeling like a nervous man about to meet the woman to whom he might become engaged. He felt both bad and good about Mrs. Kevay's saying she knew how to dress her daughter appropriately, but no amount of dress could make up for those grotesque spectacles. Maybe he could ask her to remove them. If she couldn't see, she could take his arm. He hoped Mrs. Kevay wouldn't clothe her daughter in the kind of revealing attire some young women wore. But he felt he needn't worry—that wouldn't fit with quiet Juliet who hadn't even looked him in the eye.

No, this wasn't going to work anyway, was it?

Finally, running out of time, and since this was an afternoon affair, he decided to wear casual tan slacks, a white shirt, and a brown vest. With his wavy hair still damp, he peeked into the parlor, which was empty.

Neil tapped on the bedroom door, and his grandmother called for him to come in. He stepped inside and went over to the bed where she was propped up against pillows. She laid aside a magazine and smiled at him. Yes, she looked more rested than she did most days. "Looks like your being outside in the sunshine was good for you, Grandmother."

"I feel fine," she said. "But what's this about you bringing home a guest?"

"I may be bringing a young woman home for you to meet."

Her mouth opened and her eyes widened. "Oh, Neil. Who? Where did you meet her? Why have you not said anything?"

Not wanting to be any more Machiavellian than necessary, he stated as much truth as he could. "I met her in Canaan Valley."

"Oh, tell me all about her."

He lifted her hand, conscious of how cold it felt, and warmed it with his own. "I'll let you see for yourself. If I can't have your blessing, then. . ."

"Oh, Neil. You know how happy it would make me for you to marry, carry on the McCory name. Oh my." She shook her head, and a look of pity came into her eyes. "It's about time you got over pining away for Kathleen."

He didn't think he'd exactly "pined away." Kathleen had been everything an up-and-coming young doctor could want. She was blond, beautiful, fun, educated, and the daughter of a prominent doctor in Wheeling. "Well, Grandmother, you know Kathleen wasn't the kind of woman to live here and manage the inn. It's my home, and I couldn't leave it. That's why this young woman is coming here—to find out if this is the kind of life she can live. I'm bringing Juliet—"

"Juliet?" Her eyes brightened further. "What a beautiful name. Oh, she must be lovely."

He lowered her hand to the afghan she had spread over her. "Haven't you taught me that looks aren't everything?"

"That's right. But it's. . .something. Is she unattractive?"

"Well, no. But she sort of has a. . .an eye problem."

"Crossed?" She chuckled.

Come to think of it, he wasn't sure. Maybe her eyes were crossed. That would explain why she hadn't looked directly at him—she couldn't. He had that throat-clearing problem again. "I'll let you judge for yourself."

"Well, I've had only one grandchild, and he turned out to be the most handsome man around. I'll be happy if my great-grandchildren have your looks and Juliet's lovely insides." She glanced up at him. "She is lovely inside, isn't she?"

What else could he say but, "What else but?"

She laughed and looked happier than he'd seen her look in a long time. "I know you're joshing with me, Neil. You've always been attracted to the most beautiful girls around. And they to you. I can hardly wait to see her."

Neil felt he could wait. But he'd invited Miss Kevay to the inn to meet his grandmother, and he'd see it through. Maybe Juliet wouldn't like it. Or maybe his grandmother would tell him that Miss Kevay wasn't his type.

After all, she wasn't.

❧

At 3:00, Neil pulled the buggy up to the side of the clinic where he had told Mrs. Kevay he would meet them. He parked in the spot reserved for his doctor's buggy. Either the wagon next to him belonged to Mrs. Kevay, or they were running late.

He hitched Sally to the post, thinking that it wasn't just the midafternoon sun that made him sweat. He pushed open the door, telling himself that a doctor shouldn't be having that kind of throat problem. But the kind of remedy he'd need didn't come in a little brown bottle one could buy off the shelves at the pharmacy.

He closed the door after entering the waiting room. Apparently the Kevays were running late. Carter was talking with two women. They must be new in town.

Then Carter turned, his eyes wide as saucers and his smile reaching from ear to ear. "Neil," he said. "I've just met your friends." His head was bobbing, and he seemed to have lost any other words that might be forthcoming.

Friends? Neil looked at the two women.

"Neil, you have a fine clinic here," the middle-aged woman said. "And Dr. Carter has made us feel right at home." She extended her gloved hand, and he had no choice but to take it and plant his lips on it. She had the same voice and brilliant green eyes as Mrs. Kevay, but her hair was short, curly, and red. There were no circles under her eyes nor a mole on her cheek.

"Oh, I'm so sorry. You probably don't recognize me, fixed up and all. Wigs are the in thing, you know."

Oh, so the red hair must be a wig. But it made her look more. . .citified than she had this morning. Her dress with a jacket seemed fitting for a stylish, yet conservative mother. He was almost afraid to look at the younger one who had stepped aside as if she, too, were reluctant.

"Juliet," he said with effort, taking the opportunity to catch a glimpse of her. She didn't extend her hand, and his hands were rubbing themselves together in front of his vest.

Not allowing more than a lingering glance, he, however, had the impression her white blouse had rows of lace in front and lace at the high neck and long sleeves. Kathleen dressed much fancier, but he was not looking for another Kathleen. He wasn't one to keep up with women's latest styles but thought Juliet was dressed modestly but quite acceptably for a young lady's daywear.

He dreaded looking at her face, but when he did, he felt like a weight had lifted. She was not wearing the spectacles. Her hairstyle looked quite pretty—parted in the middle and fastened in a roll from the sides of her head and curved to the back of her neck. He didn't think those little tendrils had fallen along the sides of her face this morning, but he couldn't be sure. What he wanted to see was her eyes, but she kept her eyelids lowered. He felt sure she was cross-eyed. As long as she didn't look straight at people, she'd be acceptable. He reminded himself that no one was perfect.

After Mrs. Kevay's exuberant good-bye to Carter and Juliet's quiet one, Neil nodded at Carter, who winked at him and grinned like some kind of hyena. This morning they had decided Mrs. Kevay would meet them at the Sunrise Restaurant after Juliet's visit to the inn.

When they walked around to the side of the clinic, Mrs. Kevay spoke seriously. "Neil," she said, "I've thought about this and decided I can't simply let Juliet ride away with you. After all, you are a stranger to us. We don't even know that there is a Sunrise Inn."

That shocked him. But he saw her point. "Please, Mrs. Kevay, along with your daughter, accept my invitation to the inn."

"I'd be delighted. Shall I leave Not-to-Be here?"

"Not-to—? Oh. You mean the horse? We wouldn't want to chance a horse thief coming by. You and your daughter—"

"Juliet," she corrected.

The throat again. "Juliet. You and she could ride behind me in the wagon, or she could ride with me, if you feel that is proper."

"I believe it is proper for a man's fiancée to ride with him. I'll follow."

Neil took hold of Juliet's arm just as she stepped up to get into the buggy. Her foot seemed to slip slightly, but she recovered immediately. Had she been startled by his touch? That was the gentlemanly thing to do.

"Do you have any questions, Miss. . .um, Juliet?" He thought she might ask about the town they were driving through, or his clinic, or the inn, or his grandmother.

"No, sir."

The *clip-clop* of Sally's hooves on the cobblestone street sounded unusually loud. So did the silence. After driving a bit farther, he thought a little instruction might be in order. "You do know you should address me as Neil when we get to the inn."

"Yes, sir."

He noticed she looked back a few times, as if making sure her mother was following, in spite of the obvious clunking of wagon wheels against the road.

He attempted conversation again. "You don't talk a lot, do you?" He glanced over at her.

She seemed pressed against the side of the buggy, as if afraid of accidentally touching him, and her gloved hands lay on her lap, one over the other. She did not look at him but spoke in that clear tone he had noticed that morning. "Since the job calls for me to be a companion for your grandmother, do you think she would like for me to talk a lot, or should I be less than verbose?"

Verbose? Well, she had said she went to college. Maybe she was trying to sound educated. "Just. . .be yourself," he said.

He turned his head toward her as he turned the buggy to his right. She turned her head away from him.

Yes, Juliet. Just be yourself. Your quiet, retiring, less than verbose, cross-eyed little self.

seven

Be myself?

Olivia wished she had a script to read, telling her just who "herself" was. Only a couple of days ago she'd been Olivia Easton, a motherless girl looking for a job so she could become an actress.

Now she'd become an actress before getting the job. She must be Juliet Kevay, who had a mother named Stella Kevay. Her job was to marry a stranger and pretend to be his wife but not really be his wife. So she would be pretending to be pretending to be his wife since she'd be married under the name of Juliet Kevay. They would not be legally married.

If she had anything to feel good about, that was it.

And if this doctor, who carried a Bible around with him, thought this was all right, then it must be. He was trying to give his grandmother the best year of her life by giving her hope of a granddaughter-in-law who would give him children and carry on the name of McCory.

She was doing this for a good cause, too—to make money to go to acting school so she could do what she'd been born to do. If she didn't like the grandmother, or the inn, or didn't want to go through with the marriage, then she could simply take the stand that Dr. McCory's former fiancée had taken and say that she preferred city life or felt she couldn't manage an inn.

Olivia was startled when the doctor spoke. She'd been lost in her thoughts and the rhythmic sound of wheels and hooves against the road. "Pardon?" she said.

"Our property begins here," he said and gestured toward a sign beside the road that read SUNRISE INN with an arrow pointing to the right. The horse and carriage turned to the right, and the horse gracefully clopped along the road that was bordered by stately pine and lush, green rhododendron.

They rounded a curve, and only for a moment did the large white house beyond register in Olivia's consciousness. Her attention was drawn to the people on the level stretch of lawn that looked like green velvet.

A woman and young lad were watching intently while a man knelt to show a little girl how to hold a mallet. The child, who looked to be about three years old, hit the croquet ball, and it rolled a few feet across the lawn.

A laugh of approval sounded from the doctor, and Olivia couldn't hold back her own small laugh as she remembered her father teaching her to play croquet.

"Look, Daddy. It's Dr. McCory," the lad said.

"Whoa, Sally." Neil drew to a stop as the family walked toward the carriage. The little girl had lagged behind, having picked up the orange and yellow ball. She held it close, as if it were some kind of treasure.

"My friends, the Martins, who have just arrived for a stay," Neil said. "I should introduce you." He turned to step from the carriage.

"Should I step down?" Olivia asked.

"No, that won't be necessary." He nodded to Stella who drew up beside them on the wide driveway.

"Samuel, great to see you." He walked out onto the lawn, shook the man's hand, and accepted an embrace from the smiling woman. "Melanie. And who is this tall young man?"

The boy ducked his head slightly. "I'm Chad."

"Chad? My, how you've grown. And Mary," he said when the man picked up the little girl. "You're still the prettiest girl around."

The girl grinned, clutching the ball close to her dress, and lay her head against Samuel's shoulder.

Olivia watched as they greeted each other in such a friendly manner. For a long moment, she was able to look at Neil

McCory's ruggedly handsome face, the kind she preferred over the smooth, citified type. His skin was bronzed, like he spent a lot of time in the sun—the sun that now brushed his dark brown hair with gold.

Neil introduced the family to Olivia. "This is my friend, Juliet Kevay." After their polite greetings, Neil walked them over to Stella and introduced her.

The man and woman both looked at Neil with happy faces and excitement in their eyes. Neil had not said she was his fiancée, but the sly look in Samuel's eyes and the wide smile on Melanie's face indicated they thought she was more than a "friend."

After the family returned to their game and Neil jumped up into the carriage, the horse drew them nearer the big house. While he explained the relationship to his friends, Olivia took in the impressiveness of the Federal style house nestled against the backdrop of lush, green mountains rising into the clear, late-summer sky.

"Samuel, Melanie, and I grew up together," Neil was saying. "They married and settled down in Sunrise. A midwife delivered Chad, but Melanie had such a hard time she wanted me to deliver Mary. That bonded us even more. Then they sold their house and moved to the city where Samuel is now vice president of a large bank. They come back every year to visit friends and relatives, so they stay here."

"You seem to have a way with the children," she said as he drove around the curved drive and stopped in front of the house.

"Especially with those I help bring into the world." He jumped down and came around to her side of the carriage. She already had one foot on the ground, so he took her hand as a polite gesture.

Olivia caught the whiff of some musky fragrance, possibly a shaving lotion. She thought it rather tantalizing.

Just then an elderly man came down from the porch and

said he'd tend the horses. Neil introduced him as Bart Henley.

The inn was slightly larger than her father's house in the city, and it was just as impressive with its white columns that reached to a second-floor roof and black shutters that flanked the windows. Noticing one of the black rockers moving while the others were still, she knew that's where Bart had been sitting.

She turned to see what he would see and caught her breath. The view was a family laughing and playing on that vast green lawn that stretched to the grove of stately trees that seemed to meld with the fantastic view of mountain ranges.

"That is one beautiful sight."

"Thank you," Neil said. "It's only one of many around here. God has truly blessed this area."

Enthralled by the view, Olivia hadn't realized Stella had stepped up onto the porch until her aunt touched her on the shoulder. When Olivia turned, Stella gave her a smile of encouragement.

Neil opened the screen door, and Olivia, with Stella right behind her, stepped into the spacious foyer, formed by rooms on the right and left. A staircase ran along the right wall, ending at a small landing. On the landing stood a corner table, graced by a tall vase of wildflowers. The stairway then took a sharp left, extending to the second-floor hallway. A crystal chandelier hung from the high ceiling.

"Neil, this is lovely," Stella said. "It feels like a home instead of an inn."

"That's what Grandmother wants—a home away from home for the guests."

"I suppose that's where guests check in." Olivia gestured toward the area beneath the staircase.

"Yes, it is."

She nodded, since he was behind her. "It gives the impression of someone's private library."

He laughed lightly. "I have spent some time back there, reading or writing."

Olivia could understand why. A lamp, ledger, and telephone sat on a huge desk in front of a big leather chair. Behind the chair and along the paneled walls were shelves, some with decorative items and pictures but most filled with books.

"Grandmother," Neil said suddenly, and Olivia's attention was drawn to the movement on her right.

A white-haired woman, using a cane for balance, moved slowly toward them. "Thank you for the nice compliments," she said. "And welcome to my home."

A tremor raced along Olivia's spine. She felt like turning and running. This was not just an inn, but a woman's home. This was *the* grandmother—the one who would decide Olivia's future.

As if knowing what she was thinking, Stella lightly touched Olivia's arm. The touch served as a reminder that she wasn't invading this woman's home under completely false pretenses. She was being interviewed for a job.

The elderly woman's kind smile formed deep lines in her face, which was lovely and surrounded by wavy, snow white hair brushed back into a roll at the back of her head. She was dressed in a fine pink dress with lace and buttons. A rose-colored shawl lay around her shoulders. She obviously had been a beautiful woman in her younger days. She stood shorter than Olivia or Stella and appeared rather frail, but there was something elegant and confident in her demeanor.

"I could not wait in the parlor," she said in a slightly breathless voice, like one who had walked hurriedly rather than slowly across the carpet. "I've been watching from the window."

As soon as Neil finished the introductions, the woman said, "Call me Mama McCory. Everyone does, except Neil, of course."

Olivia held out her hand. Mama McCory ignored it, handed Neil her cane, and embraced Olivia. The woman's fragrance was like sweet lavender with a faint aroma of talc or face powder.

At that moment, Olivia thought she knew something of

how Neil felt about his grandmother. Her smile was sweet, and her eyes, dark and as intelligent as Neil's, expressed love and acceptance.

Mama McCory released her and stepped up to Stella. She looked into her face for a long moment, then opened her arms to her. "Shall I call you Stella?"

"Please do. Since early childhood, even Juliet usually addresses me as Stella."

Although Olivia knew Stella said that in case she erred and called her Stella, she wondered if Mama McCory might think that much too forward.

The older woman stepped back, took hold of Stella's hands, and held them as she laughed softly. "I can imagine that was adorable when she was a little one." She looked over at Olivia then. "She's certainly adorable now. And those eyes are the most beautiful and expressive I've ever seen." She looked at Stella again. "There's no wondering where she gets them. Eyes like the two of you have are unforgettable."

"Thank you," Stella said at the same time Olivia said it softly. Both she and Stella often heard comments like that.

"Now," Mama McCory said, "come into the parlor. Hedda has gone to fetch our tea." She took her cane. Neil crooked his arm, and she wrapped her frail arm through it.

When they came to the door of the parlor, he stopped. Mama McCory walked on in. Neil gestured for Olivia and Stella to go ahead of him.

Mama McCory went to an armchair. "I like a chair with arms," she said. "That makes it easier for me to get up. Please, sit on the couch."

After they sat, Neil took a chair across from them, on the other side of the coffee table.

"Oh, this is Hedda," Mama McCory said when an older woman, wearing a long apron over her dress, came in with a silver tray and set it on the coffee table. She introduced Stella and Juliet.

"Very nice to meet you," Hedda said and straightened. She smiled at Juliet. When she looked at Stella, her breath seemed to halt for a moment. "Have we met before?"

Juliet watched Stella study the woman then smile demurely. "I can't say. Where do you think we might have met?"

Hedda shrugged. "You're not from Sunrise, are you?"

"No," Stella said, still looking at her and smiling as if waiting for another question.

Olivia knew she and Stella both would have found something like this funny at any other time. Stella was probably finding it humorous now. She simply played the part of a modest woman being questioned by the hired help.

As if realizing that herself, Hedda's cheeks pinked and she turned to face Mama McCory, who said, "Thank you, Hedda."

"If you need anything, I'll be in the kitchen." Hedda hurried from the room.

"Would you like for Juliet to pour?" Stella asked.

"Please," Mama McCory said.

Olivia looked at the silver tea set and the china cups. She'd been taught etiquette as far back as she could remember. She knew the routine. She wasn't concerned about asking if anyone preferred sugar, one lump or two, cream, or just taking it plain. She knew what to do with napkins and cookies.

Removing her gloves, however, she felt self-conscious, wondering what kind of interrogation might follow. If a servant asked a personal question, what might Mama McCory ask?

eight

Neil saw Juliet hesitate only slightly after pouring his tea last. Hoping she would get the signal to keep it plain, he said quickly, "I'll have one of those small cookies, please."

She laid a cookie on the side of the saucer, picked it up, along with a napkin, and walked over to him.

The tea sloshed over the rim of the cup and into the saucer when Juliet handed it to him. He looked up at her. He hadn't enough breath to say it was his fault—his hand was the one that shook. Earlier, when his grandmother had said Juliet had beautiful eyes, he had thought that was one of the few times she had erred like that. One shouldn't say crossed eyes were beautiful, no matter what their color.

Neither of the women had seemed insulted. Now he knew the reason why. Speechless, he stared up into the most beautiful eyes he'd ever seen. They were a deeper green and even more stunning than her mother's that had so impressed him.

He looked down quickly, holding a firm grip on the saucer, hoping it wouldn't crack under the pressure. If he wasn't careful, both his grandmother and Stella might think he was so taken with Juliet that he couldn't keep his eyes off her.

But that was what his grandmother was supposed to think, wasn't it? No doubt she would notice the color he felt rise to his face. She was an observant woman, but who could tell if the color in one's face was from some romantic emotion or from what one was feeling—humiliation and surprise?

The sound of a cup lightly touching a saucer and the faint sound of a voice and laughter on the front lawn, wafting through the open windows where the breeze stirred the lace curtains, was enjoyable. Stella appeared perfectly at ease. Juliet appeared tense. He would have thought it strange had she not appeared so.

Stella commented on the tea and cookies being quite good, and Juliet agreed, then blotted the sides of her mouth with a napkin and laid the cup, saucer, and napkin on the tray.

For a while, Mama McCory and Stella commented on the good weather they'd been having. Stella then mentioned the piano between a window and the corner. "Do you play?" she asked his grandmother.

"Not often. I have rheumatism so bad in my hands anymore. Sometimes when my fingers allow, I'll pick out a tune. But it's an effort, and my fingers don't flow over the keys like they once did."

To Neil's surprise, Stella asked his grandmother, "Would you like Juliet to play something for you?"

Neil watched his grandmother's eyes light up as she looked at Juliet. "Oh, would you, dear?"

After a moment, Juliet rose from the couch and walked to the piano. She sat with the straight back and grace of a young woman who had been trained to play in a drawing room. That reminded him of many young women he'd known, some who played well and some who played poorly.

Where would a girl who grew up in a mining town learn to play the piano? But she had been in the city, too, at college. Maybe she had learned from Stella who did not fit his picture of a miner's wife. Perhaps she and her husband had been incompatible, like he and Kathleen.

He had no idea what to expect, but he certainly didn't expect what happened after a long moment of Juliet's sitting there, poising her hands over the keyboard. She began playing "In the Good Ol' Summertime."

His grandmother couldn't conceal her pleasure. She began to nod and in her thin, somewhat trembling voice began to sing along. Stella chimed in. That woman had a good voice. Juliet didn't sing; she just continued to play while staring at the wall beyond her as if she were playing classical music in the finest of drawing rooms.

After finishing the song, she rose from the bench. His grandmother motioned for her. "Come here, dear."

Juliet walked over to her.

His grandmother's eyes were teary. Grasping Juliet's hand, she patted it affectionately. "You couldn't have played anything I liked better. That was one of my and my husband's favorite songs, oh, seven or eight years ago when we first heard it." She smiled wanly and let go of Juliet's hand. "He died six years ago."

"I'm sorry," Juliet said and touched her shoulder.

"Oh, don't be sorry about the song. Sometimes I get teary thinking about Streun McCory, but I like to remember our times together. A lot of people change the subject when I say his name, as if he should never be mentioned. I don't feel that way."

"I can understand that," Stella said. "I've lost loved ones, and I, too, prefer to recall the good times."

Mama McCory nodded and looked fondly at Stella. "You and I could have some good talks. But for now," she said, "would you like to see more of the house?"

Both women reacted warmly. Neil was glad his grandmother mentioned it. For a moment, he seemed to forget this was a time for Juliet and her mother to discover if this job was right for Juliet.

For a couple of moments, when he'd looked into Juliet's eyes, then watched her play and saw the pleasure on his grandmother's face, he too had forgotten this was about a job. Instead, he had delighted in the feeling that his grandmother liked this young woman he brought home for her to meet.

"I'll leave the tour to you women," he said. "I'll just duck out and see what's going on with Samuel and his family."

First, he went into his study, opened his safe, and took out a small box. He whispered a prayer, "God forgive me if I'm wrong."

❧

"I don't climb stairs anymore," Mama McCory said, leading Olivia and Stella from the parlor and into the hallway next to the part of the stairs that formed the landing. "Those rooms are in use now anyway." Lifting her cane, she pointed to the room on the left. "That's my bedroom," she said. "Next to it is now part of the dining room. We tell guests to use the hallway on the left to reach the dining room. We'll go this way."

Olivia and Stella followed her past the parlor. She gestured to her left. "We had this wall put in since this is our family area. Over here is Neil's bedroom," she said when they passed a closed door to the room next to the parlor. "The one next to it is his study."

She opened the door to that one. Olivia liked it upon sight. There was a patterned love seat and an ornate desk smaller than the one in the foyer. The wall was paneled halfway up to a chair railing. Above that was light beige wallpaper with a hint of a maroon-striped pattern. The curtains were maroon. It had not only a masculine look, other than the love seat, but it had a masculine smell, like that musky fragrance of Neil and leather and furniture polish.

"He has a telephone in here, too," Mama McCory said with a sense of pride.

"I'm sure he needs one," Stella said. "His being a doctor. A lot of the homes are getting them now, but I don't have one in my cabin in Canaan Valley."

Mama McCory was somewhat familiar with Canaan Valley, and they talked briefly of places they all knew. "Hedda and I used to go down there. I'd go to that bakery on Main Street, buy some of their muffins, and come back and try to figure out what all was in them."

Stella laughed as they reached the kitchen. "I used to work in that bakery. I could tell you a few things about ingredients."

"Oh," Mama McCory said, "we must talk."

Hedda apparently overheard. "That may be where I saw you."

"I don't know," Stella said. "I haven't worked there in several years." She changed the subject. "I love this kitchen. And I see you have all the modern conveniences."

Mama McCory nodded. "It's amazing we ever ran an inn without them." She sighed. "But nobody knew any different. I remember when we used wood in the stove instead of coal. And when we used to have to go to the well for water instead of it being pumped into the house. And when electricity came. . ."

"Even I remember that," Olivia said.

"Yes," Stella said, "it's amazing the progress that has been made in just a few years."

Mama McCory agreed. "Telephones—did you see the one in the foyer? Why, I can pick that up and talk to my friends anytime I want. Well, to those who have one."

Olivia got the impression that might be Mama McCory's favorite convenience until she added, "And inside bathrooms. Of course, we're more fortunate than most. For a long time I've felt it my Christian duty to share what I have with others."

Stella asked, "What do you think about the automobiles?"

"Oh, don't get me started." Mama McCory huffed. "They are a nuisance—noisy, smelly, don't go half as fast as a horse. They won't last."

Olivia didn't bother to say that horses could be quite smelly, too. Her father had a roadster and loved it. She hadn't minded riding in it, but she preferred taking a leisurely ride in an open carriage and taking in the views. Also, horses didn't tend to break down or get stuck in the mud like those horseless carriages.

Just then Neil made his appearance. "I think the cities are adjusting to the horseless carriage," he said. "But in a town like Sunrise, with the mountain roads and steep inclines, horses do a better job."

He smiled, and Olivia thought, *Is that my husband-to-be?*

"If you ladies have finished your tour, you might enjoy seeing more of the grounds," he said.

"They haven't seen the dining room," Mama McCory said. She touched Stella's arm. "If you two would like to stay over, you're welcome. We can set up a cot for Neil in his study, and you two could take his bedroom."

"We do need to get back down to Canaan Valley." Stella's voice held regret. Olivia wondered if she was pretending or if she would really like to stay here.

Olivia liked Mama McCory. She would love to be her companion. Olivia could understand why Neil loved her enough to try and give her hope in her final months.

The dining room was spacious. A long table sat in the center of the room. Four smaller round ones were placed around the room and extended to the area next to Mama McCory's bedroom. There was a fireplace, and windows on two walls.

After they thanked Mama McCory and bade her good-bye, they walked down to the stable, where Bart said the horses had been fed and watered. Neil asked if they might walk around the grounds a bit before returning to town.

I'm supposed to feel this way, Olivia told herself. *This is acting practice, so I should experience what it's like strolling along between my mother and my fiancé.* She was much more aware of that than how the flower gardens looked or the bench beneath a sugar maple.

"Mama McCory seems lonely," Stella said as they walked into a grove of apple trees where the remaining leaves shook in the breeze.

Olivia knew how those leaves felt—much like her heart did when the sleeve of Neil's shirt lightly brushed against the sleeve of her dress.

"Yes," Neil said, answering Stella. "That's one reason I want a companion for her."

"Is Hedda not a companion for her?" Stella asked.

"To a great extent. But Hedda has her husband, Bart. They

aren't here every day, and they go home at night. They would like to retire, but out of friendship and loyalty, they've stayed on. I can get temporary and part-time help, but none have ever stayed very long. Hedda is her friend," he said, "but Grandmother needs someone she feels is. . .family."

He stopped and seemed to examine a small green apple. "I could tell Grandmother liked you both." A long moment passed, and it felt like even the wind was holding its breath. Finally, he said, "Juliet, do you think you could accept the job?"

Olivia looked at Stella, who after a long moment nodded and said, "I think Mama McCory is delightful. I am in agreement if my daughter is."

Olivia knew her options. This job was a good opportunity, with the promise of more money than any job she had been able to find in the area. But there was the thought of being married to Neil, even if it was in name only—at least in fake name only.

When she didn't answer right away, Neil spoke again. "I do have two requests if you take the job. One is that you attend church with me on Sunday."

"Sunday?" Olivia said.

"Yes," he said simply. "And the other request is that you wear my mother's ring. That way everyone will know we're engaged and talk will spread."

Olivia nodded. She felt rather in a daze. The next thing she knew, they were back in the flower garden near the bench.

"Mrs. Kevay—" Neil began.

"Stella," she corrected.

He nodded. "Stella, could I speak with Juliet alone for a moment?"

"Of course," she said. "I'll wait at the stable."

When Stella was out of earshot, Neil turned to Olivia. "Would you sit down, Juliet?"

Olivia sat on the bench, then scooted over when he made a move to sit beside her. He reached into a small pocket of his vest and took out a ring. With the ring lying on his upturned palm, he said soberly, "Juliet, will you accept my. . . proposition of becoming my wife for a year?"

He smiled gently at her, and it took all her acting ability not to melt on the spot. She had to look away from his captivating dark brown eyes that seemed to dance with a golden spark. The sun winked through the branches of the sugar maple, turning the color of his hair from dark brown to honey gold.

She'd never met a man she wanted to propose to her, even though a few had alluded to it. She rather wished this were real, that she and Neil had met under different circumstances.

Staring at the beautiful diamond ring, she had that trembling feeling again along her spine. She knew that sometimes one could get caught up in a play or a book and it seemed real. That's what this felt like, as if she were really a prospective fiancée of a handsome doctor. That's what she was supposed to feel. That was the job.

Job. That's what she must dwell upon. She would be committed for a year, and then she'd have her freedom. No more fights with her father. She could live her life as she pleased.

She swallowed hard. "Yes," she whispered.

"Your left hand, please."

She untangled her left hand from her right one and held it out. The touch of his fingers did to her hand what that tremor had done to her spine. With his slight push, the ring slipped over her knuckle and seemed to be a perfect fit.

Olivia looked long into his eyes, feeling warmth travel through her body and settling in her face. She lowered her gaze to the ring. Her hand was against his as if he were holding it for her to see the sparkle of the diamond. She didn't know how it was possible to feel like two people. One was happily engaged to a handsome, appealing doctor. The other would pretend to be married to the doctor, but it wouldn't be real—just a job.

Wasn't that what acting was all about—being yourself and also being a different character? The trouble was that at times she began to feel she didn't know which one of her was the real one and which was the actress.

Neil let go of her hand, and his voice invaded her contemplation. "Thank you," he said solemnly and stood, squinting as he lifted his face toward the sky. "I'm beginning to think this is God's will for my situation."

Really? Olivia wondered at that. Then maybe God wasn't as stuffy as she had thought.

nine

"I'm not even going to think about the haste of this, Neil," his grandmother said after Juliet and Stella left in the wagon and he told his grandmother that he and Juliet were engaged. "I trust your judgment, and from all I see of Juliet, she is lovely." She smiled. "And that Stella is a delight. I really like her. I think she's very smart."

"Really?" Neil didn't say he thought so, too. But he got the feeling that Stella was in control of this whole situation and not he. But, on second thought, shouldn't a mother be the controlling one in a situation where her daughter would commit herself for a year to a man as his wife of convenience? He could only hope, when the year was out, she would not try and make trouble.

Right or wrong, he was committed, and his grandmother was happier than she'd been in a long time. That's what he wanted.

His grandmother took hold of his sleeve. "I know you had to bring Juliet to the inn, and both of you feel she can be content here. I suppose you see now that Kathleen wasn't the girl for you."

Neil nodded. If a woman could not understand his obligation to his grandmother and his responsibility to care for her in her own home, then she wasn't right for him.

On Sunday morning, Neil stood in the churchyard with several men, including Samuel and Bart. Many people walked, and some came in wagons and others on horseback.

He'd told Stella and Juliet, before they left the inn, that the church he attended was back from the first road before driving into Sunrise. There was a village, and the church would be obvious by its position on an incline and the steeple on its roof.

He was reluctant to mention his engagement to the men around him in case Stella and Juliet kept the ring and never showed up again. If so, he couldn't report it to the authorities. Who would believe such a story?

He felt a sense of relief, and shame for having doubted, when they drove up in the wagon. "My fiancée," he said.

"I expected as much the other day." Samuel gripped his shoulder. "She's a beautiful young woman."

Bart laughed. "I knew it when I saw the sparkle of that ring on her finger. But I wasn't going to say anything till you did."

Neil reached up and took Juliet's hand to balance her as she stepped down. She was not dressed as finely as Kathleen would have been. But she looked respectable and quite smart in a conservative dark blue suit and a light blue blouse. She wore a pert blue hat with a dark bow at one side. Many of the women would be more plainly dressed. He was not embarrassed to present her as his fiancée. Besides, anyone who looked into those arresting eyes, which he tried not to do too often, would find her—as Samuel had said without exaggerating—beautiful.

He took Stella's hand for her to step down. She was wearing a large hat decorated with big, colorful flowers. Her red curls peeked out beneath it. Her green suit, the color of grass, was rather fancy, too, but no fancier than the bank president's wife or the wife of Mr. Johnson who owned the general store in town. She was just. . .more colorful.

How could he ever have thought these women were plain?

Well, they had been, but after his conversation with Stella, she had said she knew how to dress her daughter like a city girl. She did indeed, and not so anyone could find fault as far as he could see.

He held out his arm. Juliet tucked hers around it, and they walked together toward the church door. Others were looking, and some whispers stopped as they passed. He nodded and thought Juliet was smiling, with her head slightly bent, looking appealingly modest.

After they entered the church, he led the way down the single aisle, then stood aside for Juliet and Stella to sit in the pew where his grandmother was already seated.

"That's a lovely hat," Stella said, moving to the end of the pew to sandwich his grandmother between her and Juliet.

"It's fine for an old lady," his grandmother said. "Mine's quiet though. I like the way yours speaks."

Neil heard Stella ask, "What does it say?"

"It says, 'I'm a leader, and I want to live life to its fullest.'"

"Are you a psychologist?"

"No. Just a wise old woman."

He liked the way his grandmother and Stella related. His glance fell upon Juliet who glanced over at him and smiled as if she had been thinking the same thing. Then her cheeks looked rosier and she looked down at her hands. Of course, she wouldn't be thinking what he was thinking then—that it was amazing how the expression in beautiful eyes tended to reach into the soul.

Trudy Simms began to play hymns on the piano, the sign for everyone to come inside and be seated. Soon Pastor Whitfield stepped up onto the raised stage and stood behind the podium.

As always, he welcomed guests and asked them to stand for introductions. Samuel's family, on the left side of the aisle, stood. So did Neil, Juliet, and Stella.

After Samuel expressed his delight at again being in the area, Neil turned slightly, since they were on the fourth row from the front. "I'm pleased to introduce Miss Juliet Kevay and her mother, Stella Kevay, from Canaan Valley. And I hope Milton back there will reserve us a table for lunch at his restaurant."

"Out of my control," Milton shot back. "You'll have to talk to the waitress."

The people laughed, but he saw nods from the members as they looked at Juliet and Stella. He'd been to many big churches in the city and had visited the bigger one in town, but he preferred this informal, friendly kind of worship place where he'd grown up. Most were simply folks with big hearts.

"I know we're all glad to see Mama McCory back with us," the pastor said. Several amens followed.

Neil shared his hymnal with Juliet, but she didn't sing. His grandmother didn't stand, and he thought it was nice of Stella to remain seated and share the hymnal.

Neil listened carefully to the sermon, wondering if God might have a particular message for him about what he was doing, but he heard nothing that confirmed or condemned.

After the service, it seemed all the women came up to welcome Juliet and Stella and to tell his grandmother how good it was to see her at church. He escaped to the front yard where he received congratulations.

Later, when he entered the restaurant with the three women, he discovered Milton had gone ahead and reserved a table for them. He particularly gushed over Mama McCory. "It's good to see you here again," he said.

"I feel like a new woman, Milton. The engagement of my grandson has put new life in me." Others came up to the table to speak and be introduced. If the whole town didn't already know of his engagement, they would know before sundown.

Later, at the inn, Neil checked his grandmother's heartbeat and thought it sounded stronger. But she was tired and wanted to rest.

He asked Juliet and Stella to make wedding preparations. He would come to Canaan Valley as soon as he could, possibly the following afternoon, to discuss the plans for him and Juliet to be married in Stella's cabin.

After the two women left, Neil felt he had done this before with his ex-fiancée. They had talked of marriage and her living at the inn. When it ended, he'd felt jilted, and from the reactions of those who knew him, they thought he had been, too. They were all right.

This time he would be legally bound for a year. Then after a year there would be an annulment that would look to others like a divorce. Although he didn't like the stigma of divorce, it would be easier because he'd planned the whole thing out.

This time emotion wasn't involved.

This time. . .it wouldn't hurt.

❧

"I now pronounce you man and wife." The pastor smiled at Neil. "You may kiss your bride."

Olivia reminded herself she wasn't really going to melt in the arms of her husband. This was act one, scene one in a play called *You're Now Mrs. Dr. Neilson Streun McCory.* Olivia turned toward Neil and felt his hand lift hers, which now felt heavy with the weight of the wedding band he'd slipped on her finger. She felt his breath and then the touch of his warm, firm lips against the top of her hand.

She lowered her hand, and the only thing she could think to do as a wife was to lift the bouquet of marigolds to her nose. Stella had thought of flowers at the last minute. She'd picked them from her bed by the front steps and tied them with a strip of white ribbon.

The pungent odor of the marigolds, thankfully, over-whelmed the musky aftershave she'd caught a whiff of when Neil had kissed her hand. She needed to keep her wits about her, and that scent seemed to steal them away.

She must surely look the part of a shy maiden as Neil expressed as much. "Pastor, we prefer our kissing to be done in private."

Olivia dared not look at Neil. She stared at Stella and saw the gleam in her aunt's eyes. She glanced at the pastor's wife whose face had turned a deep pink as she fidgeted with pulling on her gloves.

The pastor glanced at his wife with wide eyes, then coughed

lightly and said, "Um, yes, well, I can appreciate that. Young people nowadays are getting too forward. But it's a part of the ceremony. The kiss means a joining of the soul, so to be married in the sight of God, it would be a good idea. We can look the other way."

They all turned away. Olivia visualized kissing Neil and lowered the bouquet of marigolds. Oh, he would think he was kissing a skunk. Why hadn't Stella picked wildflowers? Slowly, she lifted her face toward his and then her gaze.

His eyes met hers for an instant before she saw a furrow form where his eyebrows almost met. He looked over her head. "We've. . .finished," he said after a long moment.

Finished?

The pastor turned toward them. "Congratulations to the bride and groom." He walked over to the coffee table and signed the marriage certificate. His wife and Stella signed as witnesses. "I suppose we're. . .about done here." He looked from Neil to Stella and back to Neil.

"I'll walk you out," Neil said.

After the sound of wagon wheels and horses' hooves faded, Neil opened the screen door and stepped inside. He walked over to the table, looked for a moment at the license, and picked it up. Glancing at Olivia, he said, "Thank you again, Juliet. Stella. If there's nothing else, I'll be on my way to the convention in Wheeling. I will call and leave a message at the general store if I need to get in touch with you. If you need me—"

"Yes," Stella said, "we know how to reach you at the Wheeling Hotel."

"Juliet"—he faced her—"you are legally my wife, and I will do my best to be a good husband."

"Thank you," Olivia said. "For the. . .job."

His words, "I'll return on Sunday," were accompanied by his retreating footsteps, soon followed by the sound of Sally making a hasty retreat after he unhitched her from the carriage.

Walking to the door, Olivia watched until he rode out of sight. Her husband would ride to the depot, take the train to Wheeling, and attend a medical convention. He had said he wanted particularly to visit with the heart specialists whom he had consulted about his grandmother's stroke and weakened heart.

She wondered if he would rent a carriage there or if he would hire an automobile. Had he ever driven an automobile? She didn't know a lot about this man she would pretend to be married to for a year. Something in her wanted to. Would he see Kathleen while there? If so, would he tell her about his marriage? Would he be sorry he'd done this?

Stella's voice brought her back to reality. "Throw those marigolds in the yard," she said. "They're pretty, but they sure can stink up a place."

Olivia removed the ribbon from her wedding flowers—yellow and orange marigolds. She threw them—not to a bridesmaid who hoped to be next to fall in love and marry—but into the yard where they would fade, wither, and die.

Returning, Olivia sat on the couch beside Stella and read what she'd already read twice that morning—the contract entitled "Marriage of Convenience."

The agreement was much like Neil had outlined in the newspaper ad and when he had talked with them that first morning at the Canaan Valley Restaurant. "It will be annulled after a year," she said, "and I will return the rings to Neil."

Stella didn't open her eyes. "This sounds like you've landed a good job, Olivia."

Olivia felt as drained as Stella looked. They'd both had a hectic few days, making arrangements for a wedding. Olivia hadn't wanted to wear white, so she wore a simple fawn-colored skirt and matching blouse that they felt was befitting one being married in the morning at home in a simple ceremony. Stella had gone far up the mountain to find a preacher she thought would not know her or would not have heard of Dr. Neil McCory.

Thinking Stella might be asleep, Olivia murmured, "Well, I guess I'm on my honeymoon."

All of a sudden Stella opened her eyes. "I have an idea. Let's go celebrate your marriage—I mean, your job. We can have lunch in town." She looked tenderly at Olivia. "I didn't rope you into something against your will, did I, Olivia?"

Olivia thought. "Maybe at first, but I could have backed out at any time, and you did keep saying that. There's an upside and a downside to this."

Stella sat straighter. "What's that?"

"One," Olivia said with a feeling of joy, "I can send a telegram to my father and tell him I have taken a job and am able to make a life for myself." She felt her smile fade, and she pursed her lips for a moment. "The bad part is I'll be leaving you to go and live in Sunrise."

Stella patted her arm. "We'll be closer than when you were in the city and going to college. Also, I didn't feel too welcome at your father's home. But we can see each other often at the inn. Now"—she rose from the couch—"let's hitch Not-to-Be to that carriage and go paint the town."

"But. . .what if someone from Sunrise sees me? I'm supposed to be with Neil on my honeymoon."

Stella scoffed. "Not to worry. Who would ever recognize you in the blond wig that's been lying useless in that trunk for way too long?"

Olivia was glad to laugh. She hadn't done much of that lately. "I need to wash my hands. The marigold smell is driving me crazy."

She went into the bathroom, and the light caught the gleam of the diamond ring. She stared at her hands, outstretched. Neil McCory believed she was his wife. He had kissed her hand. "Stella?"

Stella came to the doorway. "Yes, dear?"

Slowly her head turned toward her aunt. "I've had a few

boys kiss me. But I never felt anything. . .special. Can kissing. . . really be like that?"

"Depends on who you're kissing." Stella patted her shoulder. "Obviously, you haven't kissed the right person."

ten

Four days later, Neil was hitching Sally to the carriage when Juliet walked out the doorway of Stella's cabin and stood on the front porch at the top of the steps. "Hey," she said softly.

He didn't know what else to say but "Hello." Saying, "Good afternoon," would sound too formal to one's wife. "Sorry I had to call and say I'd be later than expected," he said like a dutiful husband. "I suppose you got the message?"

"Yes, Stella and I checked with the general store every day."

"The rain didn't stop for two days in Wheeling," he explained. "There was flooding, and automobiles were stuck in the mud at the sides of roads. One was stalled on the railroad tracks. Thank goodness the word got to the depot before the train left and they could get the auto off the tracks. That's why the train was delayed."

"It rained here, too, but not that much."

After his quick glance took in her appearance, he focused on Sally and the carriage. To make conversation, he said, "The carriage isn't where I left it a few days ago."

"Oh, were we wrong to take it into town?"

He glanced up. Her hand, which he had come to know was as graceful as her mother's, lay against the delicate pink lace at her throat. His gaze lingered for a moment. A ray of late afternoon sun slanted across her auburn hair and turned it to reddish gold. Her cheeks were flushed as if she thought she'd done something wrong. "No," he said. "I just noticed and. . .said it."

Relief washed over her face. "We did take it into town. I mean it's so much nicer than that creaky old wagon."

"I. . .don't mind."

"You look like you mind. Your eyes squinted and your mouth sort of looked funny."

He stared at her. "Funny?"

"Oh, I'm sorry. I don't mean ha-ha funny. I mean. . .like you're troubled."

"No. Not exactly."

"Well, if you don't want me to ever take the carriage, just tell me." Her hands fluttered in front of her. "I don't know how to act like a wife. I've never been married."

Neil quickly finished what he was doing. He walked up and propped one foot on the step. "I've never been married either. Do you suppose this is what's called—" He'd almost said, "A lover's spat." Quickly he changed it to "What's called. . .our first argument?"

After a moment of her incredible green eyes staring into his, her expression softened and she smiled. "I think it might."

He straightened and stood on both feet. "But you were right. Something did concern me. Not that you took the carriage, but that someone might recognize you."

"No, no. I wore a wig."

"A wig?"

She nodded, her face aglow with the slanting sun. "A blond one."

He tried to picture her as a blond. Kathleen was blond. Kathleen's eyes were light blue, not green. "You do that often—wear a wig?"

"No. It's Stella's. She has. . .wigs."

Neil felt himself nodding like a willow branch in the wind. The first time he saw Stella she had brown hair pulled back in a knot. The next time she had copper-colored curly short hair to just below her ears, like some of the doctors' wives wore theirs. Well, he would not concern himself with whether or not a woman wore wigs. "Is your mother in Sunrise?"

"My?" She looked as if she hadn't understood the question.

"Oh," she said after a moment. "Yes. She went up right after lunch to help your grandmother and Hedda prepare for the reception tomorrow."

He walked up onto the porch. "Let me wash up, then we should be on our way." She went inside ahead of him. After washing up, he saw that she'd put on a gray jacket that matched her skirt. The gray and pink looked nice together. "Oh," he said, "I see you're wearing those pointed shoes."

"Is something wrong with that?"

"No, no. I saw some of the city women wearing that kind."

"Stella keeps up with the latest styles." She picked up a shoulder bag and a small travel bag.

"Do you have anything else to take?" he asked.

"Stella took my luggage."

He took the bag from her, and soon they were on their way up the mountain. "Sorry to be driving Sally so fast," he said. "But darkness comes quickly once the sun has dropped behind the mountains."

"Good idea," she agreed. "After all the rain, there may be potholes in the roads. By the way, did you get to see people you knew in Wheeling?"

People I knew? Have I mentioned that Kathleen's father was a doctor? "Yes. Yes, I did."

Her asking that question surprised him. But if she went away for several days, he would certainly ask questions. After all, they are married, even if it is a marriage of convenience. "Kathleen's father was one of my mentors. He invited me to his home." He did not say that Kathleen had been most cordial, was still single, and managed a boutique in Wheeling that catered to stylish women.

"Did you tell them you are married?"

"No. No, I didn't mention it."

"Well, I suppose there's no reason. After a year, you won't be."

That surprised him, too, as if she knew his thoughts. He didn't know what he would do when his grandmother was no longer with him. "It was a good convention. And I spoke with Dr. Maynard who gave me some recent reports on stroke and heart disease. He thinks there are some new medications that might at least make Grandmother more comfortable. I also consulted with a couple of doctors who will give me information that might help ease her rheumatism."

"Oh, I hope so. I was with her for only a short while. But I can see why you love her so. She's so nice, and I would love to have a grandmother like her."

"You do," he said quickly. "That's what this is all about—making her dreams of my marrying come true, for however long—"

The sudden sway of the carriage sent them both trying to keep their balance, and for an instant he was afraid the wheel might come off or get stuck in the muddy pothole. Sally knew her business, however, and pulled them right out.

After having been thrust against his arm, Juliet straightened and emitted a small laugh. "If that had been an automobile, we'd still be back there, wouldn't we?"

He agreed. "That's why we don't have many autos up here. And I wouldn't want to get stuck on this road at night. There's not much traffic on it now that the trains run daily."

"Yes," she said, "most of the people in Canaan Valley are loggers' families. They're stripping the land, which is a concern about what will happen to the town when there are no more trees. I know that's progress, but it seems to me there should be some kind of restrictions. I've heard talk that stripping the land of trees means the town could flood when there's a hard rain."

They discussed that for a while. Neil was pleasantly surprised that she would converse about the logging or even care about it. Whatever happened to that demure little spectacled creature he met that first day? He formed an answer—the same thing that happened to that demure, middle-aged, plain mother of hers. They were. . .different. And he liked the difference.

They reached Sunrise as darkness fell. Bart appeared almost as soon as Neil helped Juliet down from the carriage. Bart hugged him and welcomed him back. "Nice to see you again, Mrs. McCory."

"Just Juliet," she said and smiled.

"Thank you, ma'am. And I'm just Bart to everybody. Don't think anybody knows my last name anymore. And I've about plumb forgot it myself. But that might be old age. I'll take care of Sally."

Neil noticed that, contrary to what Bart said, he lingered, patting Sally and talking to her. He knew the reason when he and Juliet walked up the steps to the porch. The door opened, and they were bombarded by his grandmother, Stella, Hedda, and Edith Whitfield laughing and throwing rice at them.

He and Juliet were laughing, too. She was shaking her head and trying to dig out the rice stuck in her thick roll of hair. He began to help pick the rice out and brushed some off the shoulders of her jacket. Some of the pins came out, and her hair began to come loose. Her gaze met his, and he felt his laughter catch in his throat at what he was doing.

Her laugh seemed forced this time. "Why do they throw rice at weddings anyway?" She looked around at the women.

When they all shrugged, or admitted they didn't know, Neil offered the information. "Comes from a pagan ritual. Offering grain to the gods is a. . .um. . .fertility rite." Now he wished he'd kept silent. He gave a quick laugh. "There's also a ritual of throwing shoes at a couple. No, none of that," he said when Bart laughed and reached for his shoe. He looked at the women blocking the doorway. "May we come in?"

They shook their heads.

Suddenly it dawned on him that there was another tradition besides rice throwing. Juliet's head turned toward him, and her eyes widened with understanding.

He knew this would end in an annulment, but he quickly

swooped Juliet up in his arms. She squealed, and her arm cradled his neck as if she thought he might drop her. His greatest worry was that he might not let her go.

The women stepped aside, and he carried her over the threshold, aware of how easily he had lifted her and held her. He could feel her softness against his chest, her arm over his shoulder and around his neck. He wondered if that faint fragrance was her natural odor, something like women dabbed behind their ears, or her hair that brushed against the side of his face as he set her on the floor and made sure she was balanced. He'd never seen anyone prettier as she stood there, a blush on her cheeks and her hair in disarray.

"I know why a man carries his bride over the threshold," his grandmother said, and he was grateful for the diversion. "The saying is that if she trips or falls, she'll have bad luck for years to come."

"Here are the bags," Bart said. "I'll get a broom and sweep up the rice. That gets wet, and we'll all slide down the mountain on it."

"Thanks." Neil turned to get the bags. He would not dare meet Stella's eyes. Everyone there should think he found his wife. . .attractive. Everyone except Stella, his wife's mother.

He'd dreaded what questions might be asked them but soon realized they had none. He supposed it wouldn't be fitting to ask how things were on one's honeymoon. They simply mentioned the rain, and he told of the train's delay. Soon Hedda, Bart, and Edith left.

"We can't have Stella going back down the mountain tonight, Neil," his grandmother said. "I had Bart set up that old bed that was in the attic down there in your study. I didn't think you'd mind."

"Yes, that's the hospitable thing to do. You know I don't use the study very much. We certainly should do this for Juliet's mother."

He felt a sense of relief, having supposed he would have to

sleep on the loveseat in the study or on the floor. That had to be more than coincidence. More like divine providence. God must be approving this "union" with Juliet. . .and Stella.

Later in the evening, when Juliet and Stella were unpacking Juliet's things, his grandmother took hold of his hands and stood in front of him. Her dark eyes were more alive than he'd seen them in a long time. "Oh, Neil," she said, "I know I can't live forever on this earth. But it's so wonderful having family again. This is the medicine I need. I didn't even feel my rheumatism today."

When she was ready, he listened to her heart, kissed her forehead, turned out her bedroom light, and closed the door. Next he walked down the hallway to his—no, Juliet's—bedroom.

"I'll have all my things out of here as soon as I can," he said. But for the moment, he retrieved a few items of clothing, bade them good night, and went through the bathroom between the rooms and into his study/bedroom.

Later he lay in the darkness, without any light coming through the window because the sky was overcast. Wind moaned lightly through the trees. His grandmother was right. He'd almost forgotten how it felt to have family around. Tonight had felt like family. He'd made his grandmother happy.

He pulled the quilt closer around his shoulders. Faint voices and an occasional laugh sounded from his former bedroom. For a while tonight, while going through the motions of being a married man and holding his wife in his arms, he'd almost believed it. But he dared not forget that the woman in his home, in his room, in his bed, and wearing his mother's ring was not his wife.

She was his *employee.*

eleven

Olivia sat straight up in bed. Light pressed against the curtains. "Stella, should I be making breakfast?"

Stella moaned then mumbled, "I'm not hungry. I'm not even awake." She turned to lie on her back and pull up the covers Olivia had just flung aside. Her aunt blinked several times. "You never make my breakfast anyway."

"I mean for the guests. And for Neil and Mama McCory."

Stella dragged herself upright against a pillow and fluffed out her curls. "That's taken care of. Hedda supervises things when Mama McCory can't. And there's a cook who comes in early. Your role will be to take Mama McCory's place. You're the lady of the house, not the hired help."

"But I am the hired help."

"Yes, but secretly. Openly you're the mistress of the house. As far as everyone knows, except me, you, and Neil, you're married to the doctor in this town. So you must act like it. And today, after church, you and Neil will be the celebrated newlyweds at a reception that Mama McCory, Hedda, and Edith planned for you. I've been working with them on it, too."

"Who's cooking?"

Stella laughed lightly. "Everybody. We were doing that yesterday, but all the women know if they come to the reception they bring a dish of food. They do that all the time here."

"There was a dinner on the grounds at the church in the city one time, but I never went."

Stella nodded. "The only one I went to was a church picnic in a play. We didn't get to really do it, just donned our duds and picked up an empty basket and exited the stage." She laughed. "But this is real, child. You'd better get yourself into that claw-foot tub and get ready to meet the town as Mrs. Dr. Neil McCory." She jumped out of bed. "I'll go to the kitchen and say you and Neil want breakfast in bed. How's that?"

"You're a lifesaver."

Stella grinned. "I know."

Olivia felt a strange stirring in her stomach, and it wasn't hunger. "Stella, what will I do after you leave here?"

Stella looked at her with one of her loving, serious expressions. "Olivia," she said with a note of confidence, "you will rise to the occasion."

Olivia wondered if she could rise to the occasion of being welcomed by the town as Neil's wife. At least she knew how to dress appropriately and wore the same outfit she'd worn the night before in coming to Sunrise, with the addition of a small gray hat trimmed with a band of pink ribbon and a pink bow on one side.

At church, Pastor Whitfield had them stand, and everyone applauded the newlyweds. He announced that since the weather had cleared up, the reception would be on the church lawn.

Right after church ended, most of the men went to their wagons and the women walked away. Olivia's heart sank, thinking they weren't staying for the reception. However, in the next few moments, men were setting up tables they took from their wagons. Some brought doors and set them on sawhorses. They even brought benches. By the time some women put tablecloths on the tables, others were bringing dishes and boxes of food from nearby homes.

As soon as the feast of every imaginable food was spread on the table, Edith said she and Neil must go first. They were followed by Mama McCory and Stella. Olivia kept marveling that the church members and even some townsfolk were doing this for her and Neil.

As soon as she put her plate on a table, she took off her

jacket and hat and laid them across her lap. Most of the women were dressed in plain skirts and shirtwaists. She wanted to identify with them. In a way, this reminded her of the times she wanted to play with the miners' children but her father wouldn't allow it, as if she were better than they. She wasn't, and she knew all of these people were better than she. They were not pretending.

People she'd never met came by the table where she sat to congratulate and welcome her. She was glad Stella could keep conversation lively and ongoing. It felt wonderful to be accepted as their beloved doctor's wife. But she felt guilty because it was all fake.

To her surprise, people started singing "O Perfect Love." Edith Whitfield and Stella were walking toward her, holding a tall cake. They put it on the table in front of her. Hedda brought a sheet cake and set it alongside it. Neil joined her as several men brought trays of pitchers and glasses.

Olivia began expressing her delight. She looked at Neil who had a funny look on his face. His eyes seemed to hold a warning. Had she done something wrong?

"You know the tradition, don't you?" asked Mama McCory.

Dumbfounded, Olivia shrugged. "I've seen the bride and groom feed each other a piece. Is that it?"

"Hardly," said Edith.

Stella's eyes gleamed with mischief. She knew.

"The bride and groom must kiss over the cake," Edith said. "That's for future prosperity."

Now Olivia knew what that look on Neil's face was all about. But women and men were gathering around. Those nearby were cheering them on. They began to clap in unison. Little children joined in.

Neil got on his knees on the bench across from her. "I guess we're outnumbered."

She had no choice but to make the best of this. . .job. "I guess it's my wifely duty." She got on her knees across from

Neil, braced her hands on the table, and leaned over the cake.

She closed her eyes and pursed her lips, hoping she wouldn't fall in the cake when he kissed her.

All of a sudden, she knew when it was about to happen. The sweet fragrance of cake icing was replaced by the aroma of musky aftershave, the smell of Neil's clothing. Then she felt his warm breath. Like a feather, something touched her lips. Then she felt the warm, soft, firm touch of his lips on hers. His lips didn't move and neither did hers. But as quickly as it happened, it ended.

The people all applauded. Olivia opened her eyes and saw Neil back away, so she did, too. Someone handed her and Neil glasses with small amounts of lemonade in them. While others were getting their glasses and Neil walked around to her, Olivia whispered, "What's this for?"

Her heart beat fast at the idea of kissing over the glasses. These people certainly had interesting customs.

"We'll all clink our glasses together."

"Why?"

He grinned. "To keep the devil away."

Oh dear. When the pastor lifted his glass and shouted, "To the bride and groom," everyone clinked their glasses and then took a drink of lemonade. Looking into Neil's eyes, Olivia had that strange feeling again of being his wife, belonging to him—and these people.

Maybe he should go into acting, too, because something in his eyes seemed to hold hers. She could even imagine he forgot for a moment, too, that they were pretending.

But he believed she belonged to him legally, so he could look at her as if he. . . approved of her. . .if he wanted to.

Staring into his eyes and hearing the congratulations, laughter, and people moving around, she took another sip of her lemonade. Maybe—since the devil seemed to be playing with her mind—she should ask if they might clink again.

After eating a piece of the cake that Edith cut, Olivia

started to get up with her plate. Mama McCory reached over and touched her hand. "No, you're not allowed. You're the guest of honor."

Olivia smiled and looked down. Honor? Was this honorable? It seemed so. People were happy. Mama McCory was feeling better than she had in a long time. She'd only wanted a job. But what about when this ended?

Seeing a glint of light, she realized she was twisting the diamond ring that sparkled in the sunlight. She looked up and straight into the eyes of Mama McCory. Their gazes held for a long moment. Olivia tried to conceal the feelings of guilt and concern she felt inside.

Then Mama McCory smiled. That was a sweet smile of complete warmth and acceptance from this woman who thought Olivia was her granddaughter-in-law.

Olivia smiled back, hoping Mama McCory knew she was not acting like she liked her. She didn't want this woman to die but couldn't bear the thought of her knowing this marriage was not real. That would break her heart.

Oh, and wouldn't these people all despise her when this was over?

twelve

"Mrs. McCory, will you pray for Janie?" Mary Clayton asked on Tuesday morning when Neil took Juliet with him to visit church members in the hospital. He'd removed the little girl's tonsils on Monday.

Juliet's hand played with the lace at the neck of her blouse. Her glance at him held uncertainty. He nodded, and they all bowed their heads and closed their eyes.

"God is great, God is good. Let us thank Him for. . ."

Neil's eyes popped open and his head came up. They were not at a table, getting ready to eat. They were at the bedside of a pale, six-year-old girl lying in a hospital bed.

When they'd come into the room, Mary Clayton had hugged Juliet as if she were a long-lost friend. "How sweet of you to come and see my Janie," she said. "I mean, you being a newlywed and all. I wouldn't expect you to even think of her."

George Clayton also expressed his appreciation.

Their greeting her so warmly seemed to be another confirmation that he'd done right in marrying Juliet. Neil was a doctor and a grandson, expected to tend his patients and care for his grandmother. But his "wife" showing concern was special.

Now what would they think of Juliet thanking God for "the food" at a time like this? Even if there was any food in the room, Janie couldn't eat it.

Her parents didn't look up, and Janie's little hands were folded beneath her chin. The child's smile spread across her face as Juliet continued, ". . .for this pretty little girl, with the beautiful name of Janie. Thank You for Dr. Neil who took out

81

her tonsils. And thank You for ice cream that will help make her well. Amen."

They all said, "Amen."

Mary looked hopeful. "You said she could have ice cream today, didn't you, Doctor?"

"Sure did."

George said he'd run down and get some for Janie.

Mary turned to Janie. "Now see what Mrs. McCory has done for you?"

"Please call me Juliet," she said, and Mary smiled.

Janie stretched out her arms. Juliet began to sing in a clear, musical voice, "Oh, you beautiful doll, you great big, beautiful doll. Let me put my arms about you. I could never live without you. Oh, you beautiful doll." Then she put her arms around the little girl, who was obviously charmed by her.

"You were wonderful with Janie and the other patients," Neil said after they left the hospital and headed for the clinic.

"I wasn't sure what to do. But I remembered you told me to 'be myself,' so that's all I could do."

"Yourself is. . ." What could he say? Surprising? Beautiful? Admirable? He decided on, "good enough."

Since the clinic wasn't full of patients, he could take his wife to lunch. He felt good walking down the sidewalk with his smartly dressed wife. Passersby nodded or spoke.

If he had to say so himself, when they stopped for her to admire some purses in a shop window, he thought the reflection of that couple was quite handsome. She wore her tailored suit and a pert little hat with a feather in the band where the brim turned up. The gentleman accompanying her looked dapper in his suit coat and tie.

"Oh, I love that one." She pointed to a small black bag adorned with jewels.

"You want it?"

He watched her reflection as she studied the purse for a long moment. "I'm saving my money."

He wondered what for but had no right to ask. "I would be glad to. . .get it for you."

"No," she said quickly and turned from the window.

"Sorry." Of course a man shouldn't offer to buy a gift like that for a lady unless they were engaged or married. Knowing what to do or say at times wasn't easy. He was bound by a marriage license but also a legal contract saying the marriage was a temporary one in name only. She was not really. . .his.

Hesitantly, he asked, "You will allow me to treat you to lunch, won't you?"

His heart skipped a couple of beats when she looked up at him and smiled, like a lady being courted by a gentleman. "I'd be delighted."

After Milton brought their food, Neil said, "Would you say the blessing?"

"Sure."

With bowed head, he peeked as she said, "God is great. God is good. Let us thank Him for this food. Amen."

"Amen," he said, unfolding his napkin to put on his lap.

"Why are you grinning like that?"

He looked across at her. "I'm happy."

Seeing the skepticism in her gorgeous green eyes, he ventured to ask, "Are you?"

She picked up her fork. Mischief lay in her glance before she looked down at her plate. "Who wouldn't be with green beans and red potatoes staring us in the face?"

❧

Olivia looked out the kitchen window when she heard the sound of wagon wheels against the cobblestones. "It's Stella." She hadn't seen her in three weeks, but it seemed like a lifetime.

"Run out and see what she's up to," Mama McCory said. "I would, if I could run."

Olivia laughed, rushed outside, and hugged Stella. "I'm so glad to see you. I didn't know you were coming today."

"Two reasons," Stella said. "Good news and not-so-good news."

"Something happened?"

"No. Just a letter from that stubborn ol' brother of mine."

Olivia groaned. "My father. What's he done now?"

Stella took a letter from her pocket. "I didn't read it. But knowing Herman, it won't be good." She handed the letter to Olivia. "But the good news is that I called your dad's housekeeper and asked her to send some of your personal items and clothes. I thought you'd need mainly skirts and shirtwaists."

"Thank you." Olivia tore open the envelope and read aloud.

Olivia,

I've always wanted the best for you. I'm sorry we don't agree on what's best. Apparently you will no longer listen to me, but to your aunt Stella. You must learn your lessons the hard way. I hope you will come to your senses and realize an acting career is not right for a young lady.

I can't imagine what kind of job you've taken since you didn't say. Maybe one like Stella, playing in a honky tonk. Was your college education and good upbringing all a waste?

Sorrowfully,
Your father

"Oh, honey," Stella consoled.

"It's all right." Olivia stuffed the letter into her skirt pocket. "I've felt rejected by my father since I first mentioned acting. Let's go inside, where I'm accepted for my acting ability."

Olivia loved the way Mama McCory took to Stella. The two of them sat at the kitchen table, sipped coffee, and talked.

"Juliet is becoming quite a cook." Mama McCory cast an approving glance at Olivia.

"What? Juliet a cook?"

"See for yourself." Olivia took the Peace Brunch Pie from the icebox. She cut Stella a piece, and after one bite, Stella agreed it was wonderful. Mama McCory decided to have a small piece, although she'd already had breakfast.

"Not only is Juliet learning to cook, and not just breakfast," Mama McCory said, discussing her as if she weren't there, "but she's learning to manage this inn. Still, she does have a problem."

Olivia caught her breath. What was she doing wrong?

Stella looked concerned, too.

Mama McCory took a sip of coffee to wash down the pie. "She has trouble giving instructions to our cleaning ladies. When Juliet sees something that isn't dusted or cleaned well enough, she does it herself."

Olivia smiled at that. Her father had a housekeeper and a cook. They knew their jobs, and he was great at giving orders. She walked over to get their empty plates. "I don't want to run them off. You and Neil, and Hedda, too," she said, taking the plates to the sink, "have talked about the trouble you've had keeping workers."

"Everything is running smoothly," Hedda said, beginning to wash the plates, "now that you're here."

Maybe it was her imagination, but Olivia felt there was an edge to Hedda's voice. It was accompanied by a sidelong look at Stella. A small silence followed. Mama McCory seemed not to notice.

In case Hedda was simply complimenting her, Olivia said, "Thank you."

Stella, however, looked directly at Hedda. "Does that mean you'll be retiring soon, Hedda?"

Hedda scrubbed the plate harder than necessary. "When I'm sure Juliet has learned enough. She's doing a good job, but she's still new at it."

Olivia pretended to be looking at a recipe for a dish she wanted to try. Hedda didn't mean anything by using the word "job," did she? No, of course not. Everybody said things like that.

"You have a point," Mama McCory said. "Juliet is still a newlywed. With her learning all this and Neil doctoring, they don't have much time together."

"You are so insightful, Mama McCory," Stella said. "She and Neil should take a day off."

Olivia told herself that the expectation welling up in her was simply excitement over getting out and seeing more of the spectacular views of these panoramic mountains, not anticipation of being alone with Neil. But they were supposed to be giving the impression that they were a married couple.

Stella and Mama McCory kept making their plans.

"Carter is on duty at the clinic on Saturdays," Mama McCory said.

"A good time might be when the leaves are at their peak."

"But that's our busiest time, Stella," Olivia responded.

"I can cook, change beds, do laundry, and clean house. And I'd love to be up here when the leaves peak. I do have something to do Friday afternoons in Canaan Valley, but I could come after that."

"Oh," Hedda said, just as the plate she was drying slipped out of her hands and thumped onto the rug in front of the sink. She examined it. "It's not broken. I'm so clumsy today."

Mama McCory waved her hand. "No bother, Hedda. Over the years, you and I both have broken enough dishes to make up several sets."

Hedda nodded and smiled. She set to washing the plate again.

Mama McCory returned her attention to Stella. Hedda came over to finish going over the recipe with Olivia. She said softly, "You make Mama McCory happy."

Olivia thought Hedda's eyes were watery. "Thank you." She could imagine that Hedda would be sad to leave the inn—and Mama McCory. Wouldn't anybody?

Olivia joined them at the table. "Now, have you two finished planning my life?"

Laughing, Mama McCory patted her hand. "For now. You and Neil must get away when the leaves are at their peak."

"I'll come that Friday evening," Stella said, "weather permitting. I'll stay for the weekend and go to church with you on Sunday."

Mama McCory leaned toward Stella. "Did Juliet tell you she's playing the piano for the church now?"

Stella's "No" sounded more like disbelief than response to a simple question.

Mama McCory told the story. "Trudy didn't show up for church two Sundays ago. We found out later she was ailing. When Pastor Jacob asked if anybody wanted to volunteer—"

"She volunteered me," Olivia interrupted, and the three of them laughed.

"Well, I've heard you play," Mama McCory said. "Most of our members haven't had the opportunity to learn. When Trudy came back, she heard that Juliet had played in her place, and she wanted to sit and listen. After she listened, she said she would play the opening music and Juliet could play the hymns."

"How nice," Stella said in an exaggerated tone. "My sweet girl playing the piano in church."

"Stella plays better than I do." She decided to play a little of her aunt's game. "Why don't you come up this Saturday, stay the night, and play for us in church on Sunday?"

"Oh, please do," Mama McCory said, looking expectant.

"I'd love to come up but not play. I play by ear, not notes."

"How does that work?" Mama McCory asked curiously.

"I can hear a song," she began to explain, "and the tune stays in my mind. My fingers and that tune work together when I sit at the piano. Sometimes I can play the tune the first time. On more complicated pieces, I might have to pick it out or hear it more than once." She shrugged as if that were simple. "But once the key matches what's in my mind, my fingers know what to do."

"Amazing," Mama McCory said. "Before you leave today, I want to see Juliet play from my sheet music or the hymnal and watch you do that."

Olivia knew that Stella had heard and played church songs in some of her performances. "Yes, you should play for us Sunday, instead of me."

Olivia felt Stella's hand find her arm beneath the table and pinch it.

thirteen

On Sunday morning, Pastor Whitfield greeted them at the church door. "So pleased to see you again, Mrs. Kevay." He smiled broadly. "Your daughter is a gift from the Lord. She's the best pianist we've ever had." He put his finger to his lips and cast a furtive glance around. "Don't tell Trudy I said that."

Mama McCory laughed lightly. "Juliet says Stella plays even better than she does."

Stella protested, like one too modest to admit her talent.

"It's true," Olivia said.

"Please play for us," he said. "God gives us talents to be shared." He looked beyond them, so they moved on. Mama McCory stopped to speak to another woman.

"How could you do this to me?" Stella said. "I didn't think Mama McCory would remember your talking about that."

"Mama McCory doesn't forget a thing. Besides, don't worry. If I can act like a wife, you can act like a church pianist."

Stella stood for a moment and listened to Trudy. Then she smiled broadly and strutted down the aisle to take her seat.

After Trudy finished, Olivia walked up and sat on the piano bench. Pastor Whitfield took his place in the pulpit and looked out over the congregation.

"You all know how pleased we are that the Lord has provided us with Mrs. McCory, a gifted pianist. Well, this morning, after she plays our first hymn, we have another treat. Her mother will honor us with some special music. Now, let's turn to page 158, stand, and sing 'Nothing but the Blood.'"

When they finished, Stella walked up. "Kind of slow, wasn't it?" she whispered as Olivia rose from the bench.

Oh dear! Olivia felt like a pitcher of cold creek water had been poured over her head. For an instant she froze, seeing Stella's hands poised over the keys. What had she gotten them into? Before Olivia could return to her place between Mama McCory and Neil, the rafters were already ringing with a rousing rendition of "Mine Eyes Have Seen the Glory."

Stella's whole body was into it, and her fingers were playing notes in between any notes that had ever been written for that hymn. Olivia knew that would be a hit for an outdoor crowd—even in a nickleodeon. But in a church?

Was Stella ruining everything? She was supposed to be the mother of Juliet Kevay McCory, the respected wife of the town's beloved doctor.

This should light a fire under the members any minute. The first movement was a woman's head turning. Then she saw that the woman was Hedda, with eyes popping and mouth agape.

Olivia was afraid to look at Neil. He must be terribly embarrassed. Pastor Whitfield sat in his chair on the platform, staring at Stella like she was one of the great wonders of the world. In fact, Olivia reckoned she was.

Not only were the rafters ringing, the pew seemed to be shaking. Feeling like people were looking at her, too, Olivia peeked to her left. Mama McCory was shaking while covering her mouth with her hand. Was she laughing? Well, becoming the laughingstock might be a little better than being tarred and feathered.

Stella was almost bouncing off the bench.

"Hallelujah!" came a voice from the back. A couple of male voices roared, "Amen!" A woman said, "Praise the Lord!" A woman down front stood and lifted her arms toward the ceiling. Then one on the other side of the aisle did the same. Heads were bobbing and bodies were bouncing.

"More, more," someone yelled when she finished with a flourish. Stella slapped her hands on her thighs and faced her audience with a look of triumph while they said amen and applauded. Olivia wondered if Stella had led them down the path of wickedness and turned this place into a honky-tonk.

Pastor Whitfield walked a few steps over to the piano with his hands outstretched. "Please," he pled. "One more."

A wide smile spread across Stella's glowing, beautiful face. "Everybody," she shouted and began pounding out a fast version of "When We All Get to Heaven." They all stood, began to clap and sing and sway—except Hedda. Then Bart poked her and she stood. Before long, she was moving, too.

Even Mama McCory was standing, clapping, and singing. Olivia looked at Neil. His gaze met hers, his eyebrows lifted, but he grinned then and stood, so she did, too. Soon the two of them joined in.

Amid applause and Pastor Whitfield's high praise, Stella returned to her seat. Mama McCory reached over and held Stella's hand for a long time.

Pastor Whitfield said that was a hard act to follow. It was indeed, and Olivia didn't know what his sermon was about. Her concern was what Neil might say. Although it had been entertaining, he might banish both her and Stella from his home and his sight.

After church ended, while Stella was being surrounded by adoring fans, Mama McCory held on to Olivia's arm and leaned around to speak to Neil. "Neil," she said, "let's invite Edith and the pastor to have lunch with us."

"You must be feeling better," he said. Earlier she'd said she probably wouldn't eat out.

She gave a short laugh. "I've been revived."

His brief nod seemed to say he knew what she meant. Olivia, however, felt rather drained. She turned her attention to Mary Clayton who walked up with little Janie. Neil said he'd go speak to the pastor. Several others came up, raving about how much they enjoyed Stella's playing.

Olivia was grateful for the compliments, but she couldn't keep from glancing at the aisle where Hedda had a grip on

Mama McCory's arm. Finally, Mama McCory shook her head, then turned and hastened away, quite quickly for a woman with a cane.

Hedda shot a glance at Olivia, making her wonder if Hedda had disapproved of Stella's playing.

Then she looked at her aunt, the center of attention. Yes, being around Stella was like watching a play all right—one in which you couldn't predict the ending.

&

Milton had a table reserved for them by the time they reached the restaurant. "I'm glad to have such talented ladies in my establishment." He smoothed the apron he wore over his church clothes. "Dessert's on me."

They thanked him, and waitresses brought the food. The Sunday meal was family style. Soon the table was filled with fried chicken, rice, gravy, biscuits, green beans, mashed potatoes, sliced tomatoes, and pickled cucumbers.

"Nothing against your preaching, Jacob," Mama McCory said after the pastor asked the blessing, "but it's about time we got some life back into our church. I remember when there was shouting and even some fainting when people felt the presence of the Lord."

He agreed. "You're right, Mama McCory. We need to get people more excited about the Lord than they are about the new telephones, automobiles, and running water."

Olivia's glance swept over Neil's face and sort of settled on those firm-looking lips of his. She tried to turn her mind to things of the Lord. But exactly what was she supposed to think about the Lord?

"I think the Lord was speaking to me this morning," Mama McCory said. "Again, no reflection on you, Jacob. But when Stella was playing, all we could do was just feel the music."

"I know what you mean." The pastor passed the food. "In church is a time for the Lord to speak, and it's not always through my sermon. Anyway, I'm kind of used to you speaking your mind."

"I liked your sermon," Stella said. "You talked about many things I'd never thought about."

The pastor seemed to bask in her praise. "Thank you. That's quite a compliment."

"Yes," Edith said. "Jacob and the Lord do sometimes speak in mysterious ways."

Olivia liked the way the pastor and Edith looked at each other then—he with a warning look and she with mischief. They all laughed. Olivia liked the throaty sound of Neil's laughter.

"Now that my wife has insulted me, let's move on," the pastor said. "What did the Lord say to you, Mama McCory?" He bit into a chicken leg.

"You know, after my Streun died, I quit hosting the Bible studies. Then when I thought I would start them up again, I had that stroke. I felt like life was over for me." She took a deep breath, put down her fork, and reached over to hold Olivia's hand. "There's new life in my house now." Her eyes grew moist.

Olivia looked at Neil. This is what he wanted. He sometimes glanced at her or looked for a brief moment, but this time their gazes held long enough that she saw the warmth and gratitude in his brown eyes. He finally looked down and poked his mashed potatoes with his fork.

Stella smiled at her fondly and gave her a slow wink.

Yes, it did appear she was doing her. . .job. . .well. But it wasn't just a job. She loved Mama McCory, and she didn't know a finer man than Neil.

"Mama McCory," Edith said, "do you want to start the Bible studies again?"

"If you will teach it."

Edith clasped her hands over her heart. "Oh yes. And there are so many ladies in the church who need this. We can announce it next Sunday. Then you want to start it on the following Tuesday?"

Mama McCory said she would. "Could you come up for the Bible study, Stella?"

"I would love to," she said so sincerely that Olivia suspected she meant it.

"Oh, this is wonderful," Edith said. "Should we have Juliet suggest our first topic?" The women agreed.

"Do you have a topic you'd like studied, dear?" Mama McCory asked.

"Yes," she said without having to think. "The Holy Ghost."

fourteen

Rain had fallen last weekend. Olivia feared it might again and Stella wouldn't be able to come. This Friday the weather was sunny, however, and the cooler mid-October temperatures had turned the West Virginia mountains into a spectacular array of red, gold, and yellow. The leaves were at their peak in color.

Stella hadn't been able to attend the first Bible study on Tuesday as the weekend rain made much of the road from Canaan Valley too muddy for travel. So Olivia was relieved when her aunt arrived at the inn shortly after sunset.

Hedda and Bart had left early to get home before dark, so Juliet served Stella, Neil, Mama McCory, and herself a piece of pineapple upside-down cake.

"I don't normally eat a lot of sweets before going to bed," Mama McCory said, "but Juliet is cooking up such good things nowadays. And, too,"—she reached over and patted Stella's hand—"when you visit, I don't want to miss a thing. There's always something new." She laughed. "You're wearing a tie."

Stella touched the green silk tie at her neck. "It's the style for women."

"Yes, I've noticed that. Amazing what is in the papers nowadays."

As if he, too, were thinking about another ad, Neil said, "I'm glad you're back to reading the papers again, Grandmother."

"I didn't have a reason to for a long time, Neil. When you're dying from a stroke and have a weak heart, that kind of becomes your world. Things have changed."

Stella returned her smile with her own affectionate one. "I'm sorry I didn't get to the Bible study."

"We had eight women," Mama McCory said. "Met in the parlor and had a good lesson and discussion."

"Maybe you could give me a summary of what you learned."

Mama McCory's eyes seemed to light up. "I'd love to, but first we must help clean up in here."

"There's not much to do," Olivia said. "You two go ahead. It won't take me any time to do this."

"Thank you, dear." Turning to Stella, Mama McCory said, "Let's retire to the parlor for our discussion so we'll be out of the way." The two women headed out the door, talking about the Bible class.

Neil stayed in the kitchen and helped Olivia clean up, although she protested.

"I'm glad to help, Juliet. You're busy from before sunup to late at night."

"I'm busy, yes," she agreed. "But it's not hard work. Anything I can do for Mama McCory is not work but a pleasure."

"That's fine," he said. "But I'm glad Stella is here and said she will help with breakfast in the morning. I'd be pleased if you could spend more time with the things you like to do. Like cooking, Bible study, playing the piano, reading. . ."

"I do those things," she said, handing him a plate to be dried.

"Good," he said. "I don't ever want you to feel like you're just. . .anything less than my wife."

Olivia let go of the plate and stuck her hands back into the soapy water. There was only one time each week when she felt less. And that's when he gave her the dollar she'd earned.

❧

Neil thought she might say, "You decide," when he asked what she'd like to do on their day off that his grandmother and Stella had planned for them.

She responded, however, with a great deal of enthusiasm. "Could we take a hike? Everything is breathtakingly beautiful right here. But I'd like to see more. Fall is my favorite season."

"Mine, too." Neil liked finding out what she enjoyed. Maybe on this day off they could get to know each other better.

"Will we hike all the way to the top of the mountain?"

He laughed. "I think we'd better ride Sally. At least part of the way. It's a long way up there."

Her face was animated. "I'll make a picnic lunch." He felt rather pleased that she seemed to eat the rest of her breakfast with a great amount of zest, as if she couldn't wait to begin their day's adventure.

Yes, like his grandmother had said several times over the past few weeks, "Juliet's and Stella's enjoyment of life could be quite contagious."

He sat for a while longer, sipping another cup of coffee and stealing glances at Juliet making sandwiches for their lunch. If he did have a wife in the true sense of the word, he wouldn't want her thinking he'd married her only to manage an inn and be a companion to his grandmother. He would want to take time to show her that he. . .cared.

Then he should do the same for Juliet. After all, they were legally married.

Thirty minutes later, Neil stared at the young woman who walked out the back door wearing a shirtwaist much like she wore daily, a riding skirt, and sensible hiking boots. She came up to him and Sally. Her auburn hair was pulled back from her face and was fastened with a wide clasp at the back of her head. It hung in waves to below her shoulders. He envied the early morning sunshine that caressed it with a touch of reddish gold.

With the discipline of a doctor trained not to say everything on his mind, he reached for the bag of lunch she'd prepared and fastened it to the side of the saddle. He mounted the horse, then looked down at her. "You can ride in front and I'll look over your head so we both see the views. Or you may ride behind me and stare at my back."

Her gaze moved toward heaven as if that were a ridiculous statement. Laughing, he hoisted her up in front of him. They rode along a trail marked for the inn's guests and tourists. A young couple moved aside to let them pass.

Olivia glanced around at him. "You think the hikers will appreciate a horse on the trail?"

"No, I don't." A short distance ahead he did what he'd intended all along. He left the trail, and Sally trotted along a familiar path.

Soon he stopped, dismounted, and held up his hands for Juliet. She gave him a questioning look, but he grinned at her and tied Sally to a tree limb in the completely wooded area. "This way." They walked onto a trail where they could peek through the myriad colored trees on their left and see the town below. On the right was the steep mountainside.

He heard the trickle of water about the time Juliet spied it and laughed gleefully. Water flowed over an outcropping of rocks like a miniature waterfall and formed a pool at the side of the trail. They cupped their hands and drank the cold, clear water.

Farther on, as the trailed curved up and around the slight incline, they passed others who were strolling along, enjoying the beauty of the day and the scenery.

She stopped. "Look how dark it is up there on that section of the trail."

"Look at this," he said, picking up a stick. He pointed with it to a muddy place on the side of the trail. "What kind of track do you think that is? Bear? Mountain lion?"

Her eyes widened. "Are you trying to scare me?"

"Yeah." He grinned at her.

She hit him on the arm and marched toward the dark, casting a glance over her shoulder that dared him to follow. He had no problem doing that. She slowed upon reaching the path into the section where rhododendron formed a canopy, allowing very little light into the area.

"There really are bears and mountain lions around here, aren't there, Neil?"

"Yes, but they try to stay out of our way."

All of a sudden something was upon them. Juliet let out a yelp, and Neil pulled her close to the side of the path and jumped out of the way. A young man apologized and kept running. That's when Neil thought he should take Juliet's hand in his, which he did. She didn't protest, but they let go when they walked into the light again.

They wound up and around, then stopped for a moment to look down, able to see the town that now looked even smaller.

Neil explained that the trail was almost parallel to the one they'd hiked. "We'll soon be back down to Sally."

Sally snorted, as if showing her disapproval of having been left in the forest. They mounted her, and after a time of winding up through the woods, the trees thinned. A sudden gust of wind whipped the tree branches, and soft yellow leaves fell on them like pieces of gold and blanketed their path.

Juliet held out her hand and laughed with delight. Suddenly her breath caught and all she could say was, "Oh."

That's how Neil felt whenever he came here.

They dismounted. While she walked toward the spectacular view of mountains below and beyond them, Neil secured Sally. He spread the saddle blanket out and set the bag of lunch on it, then walked up to Juliet.

"I've never seen anything so beautiful," she whispered, as if a voice might disturb the scenery. She looked over at him. "The colors, too, are more vivid than I've ever seen."

Hearing her appreciation of this spot that meant so much to him and looking into her eyes, he said, "Green is beautiful, too."

She blinked her eyes and looked again at the scenery. "I'm sure it's beautiful here anytime. And the town below is like a toy town."

Feeling he had made an error in implying something too personal, he turned and walked to the blanket. She followed, and soon they were eating the sandwiches, fruit, and cheese, and drinking from the canteens. All sounds were magnified. He could hear his own chewing. Sally whinnied, and he tossed his apple core for her to eat. Then Juliet did the same and quipped, "She didn't even have to step aside to get mine."

He straightened, pulling his knees up and hugging them. "Oh, was there a contest?"

"Yeah," she teased. "In case a bear shows up, somebody has to be able to hit him between the eyes."

Neil breathed easier, feeling that had eased the tension he had felt. "I've thought of building a house here someday."

She seemed surprised. "You don't plan to live in the inn?"

"Having the inn is grandmother's dream, not mine. I would like to have a home where friends can visit, but I'd like my home to be just for my family. Sunrise is becoming more of a tourist area every year. Hotels will be built. The town will become a city before long."

Juliet agreed. "The automobiles will come, too. Do you not want one?"

"They are the way of the future, contrary to what some are saying. The cities are filled with them. But for now, when I make house calls, the horse and buggy serves me better than an automobile. For one thing, we don't have the roads for them here."

"With a clinic and a hospital in town, I wouldn't think you'd make many house calls."

"I don't make a lot of them. But some of the people back in the mountains don't trust hospitals and clinics. That doesn't mean they shouldn't have a doctor caring for their needs."

Juliet looked out toward the spectacular view that went on for miles. "Has Kathleen seen this?"

"Yes." He closed their canteens and put them into the bag. "She still prefers the city."

Juliet stood. "But maybe she will prefer this when Sunrise becomes a city."

Neil picked up the blanket and shook it. "I don't think I

want to marry a woman who rejects me because I won't live in the city." He laughed as if it didn't matter. "Maybe I could. . . hire a wife."

She walked alongside him toward Sally. "I think you already did that."

"Yes, but it's temporary."

"Right," she said. "If it wasn't, I wouldn't be getting paid. Humph." She stomped her foot. "Not only are women not allowed to vote, but they don't even get paid for all the housework they do."

Neil chuckled when she grinned. He could imagine her and Stella marching and speaking about a woman's right to vote. But more on his mind was her talking about getting paid for housework.

He'd hoped to find a way to ask if she might think of him not as an employer, but as one interested in her personally. He'd shared something of his future plans with her. Surely she would know he would not do that with a woman unless he thought her. . .special.

But he'd hired her to do a job and was paying her. It wouldn't be proper to pay a woman he was courting.

This was a predicament.

He thought of the Bible studies they'd started at the inn. If ever there was a time when he needed to study his Bible and pray, now was that time.

fifteen

The end of October brought fall rains, flooded areas, and winds that almost stripped the deciduous trees bare of their brown leaves. After the cold spell, the November sky cleared, leaving a crispness in the air.

Olivia was delighted, along with Neil, that Mama McCory wanted to make big plans for the holiday season that was quickly approaching. They spent many hours poring over recipe books and discussing how to decorate the inn.

Olivia was grateful that Stella had been invited to the inn for Thanksgiving and would join them for the Thanksgiving Day service at church.

After the special service, Edith and Pastor Whitfield joined them for dinner at the inn.

The inn smelled like roasted turkey, giblet gravy, yeast rolls, corn bread dressing, nutmeg, cinnamon, pumpkin pie, cranberry sauce, green peas, and buttery corn.

"I love the smell of Thanksgiving," Mama McCory said. "It's been a few years since we've cooked a turkey and all the trimmings. I have so much to be thankful for this year."

"I've missed these invitations to your dinners, too." Jacob frowned. "To not be alone, Edith and I had to go to Milton's at Thanksgiving or depend on some church member to invite us."

"But you don't look like you've missed a Thanksgiving dinner or any others for that matter," Mama McCory quipped. "No offense, Jacob."

"None taken." He patted his ample belly, smiled broadly, and reached for the gravy bowl.

Edith sighed. "Christmas will be here before we know it."

"Oh, I'm looking forward to it this year," Mama McCory

said. "Why don't we go against tradition and decorate the day after Thanksgiving?"

"We could do that," Olivia said. "If you want to."

"Yes, we could, couldn't we? We've already planned how we want to decorate. And maybe Stella could stay and help."

"As long as you need me or want me. I don't do any more than put up a small tree with a few baubles and set out a few candles. But some years I went to my brother's house."

Olivia remembered when Stella came to their house, dressed so beautifully. The two of them would go shopping downtown. They'd have fun, walking in the snow in their boots with fur-lined hoods around their faces. Stella would make hot chocolate when they returned to her father whose glass of Christmas cheer hadn't cheered him.

"It's a shame you have to stay down there all winter," Mama McCory said. "Do you have electricity?"

"No, but it's expected to reach that far in the spring."

Mama McCory scoffed. "You could freeze to death by then." She stared at Neil. Olivia watched them communicate without speaking.

The expression in Neil's eyes was warm. He smiled and gave a brief nod of understanding. Then he looked at Olivia. "My wife is the one to interview the hired help. Maybe she has something in mind."

Oh, Olivia could have kissed him.

No. . .she supposed she couldn't. . .or shouldn't.

"Mrs. Kevay," she said as dramatically and formally as she could, trying to hold back her excitement, "we have a position open for the winter. You may have free room and board in exchange for—" She paused and cleared her throat, waiting for everyone to look at her. "In exchange for your keeping the commodes clean."

They all laughed.

Stella said, "Honey, for the privilege of staying here with you wonderful people, I would keep the outhouses clean."

They laughed again. Stella and Olivia got up and hugged Mama McCory, then they hugged each other.

Olivia looked at Neil and mouthed a sincere "Thank you."

His gaze made her feel as warm as freshly baked bread. Edith Whitfield's voice finally got her attention. "Would you do that, Juliet?"

"Pardon?" She returned to her seat. "I didn't hear that."

"Oh, good. We all have just volunteered you and Stella to be in charge of the children's Christmas program."

She began to protest.

Edith wouldn't hear of it. "You must use your talents for the Lord."

"It's your Christian duty," the pastor added.

Olivia and Stella stared at each other. Since he put it that way, what recourse did they have?

As if that were settled, Mama McCory said, "Stella, you're part of the family, so there's no way you can stay in one of the servants' rooms on the lower floor. You can have one of the guest rooms upstairs."

Stella had a different idea. "That's so far from everything though. Why don't I take Neil's study? That way I'm close to the kitchen and dining rooms. Besides, I'll be getting up early." She grinned at Neil. "I doubt he does much studying in there anyway."

Olivia thought he looked like he'd just been put out in the cold.

Finally, Neil found his voice and some color returned to his face. "That's fine. She's right. I don't really study in there." More color was in his face now. "I have my clinic, the parlor, the foyer"—he raised his hands and his eyes—"the second floor."

"Or even the lower floor with the laundry room and hired help," Stella said.

Neil grinned. "Now we know what it's going to be like, living with my mother-in-law."

They all laughed. Olivia loved the way Stella and Neil could tease each other.

&

For a long time after the guests left and everyone had retired for the night, Stella and Olivia couldn't stop giggling.

"Did you see Neil's face when he thought I was taking his secret 'bedroom'?" Stella said.

"It was priceless," Olivia agreed.

"I think it finally dawned on him that he would still have his study as his bedroom and I'd be in here with you."

Olivia couldn't be happier about that. Sitting in bed eating popcorn, their conversation turned serious.

"What do you know about children's Christmas programs?" Stella asked.

Olivia thought. "I know Father sent gifts to the miners' children on Christmas. We had our own Christmas alone. Then after we moved to the city and before I went off to college, we went to some programs at church. I remember the choir sang and the preacher preached."

"About what?"

"I don't remember. But I do remember, as we left, everyone was given a paper bag filled with an apple, orange, some nuts, a candy cane, and some hard candy."

"If that's all you remember, it must have been boring," Stella said seriously.

"Well, I liked the candy."

They each tried to remember how much they knew about church.

"We can't ask the church members here. They'll think we're heathens."

Stella nodded. "Herman made me feel like I was not as good as church people, so I never went much."

"Father and I didn't go often," Olivia said. "There was only a traveling preacher when we lived at the mining area. Before she died, Mama told me about God and even read the Bible.

But I remember very little of it."

"Your grandmother was like that. Mama McCory reminds me a lot of her. She used to talk about God like He was her friend."

After a thoughtful moment, Olivia said, "Pastor Whitfield said anybody can come to Jesus and that God invites anybody and we are to tell others that."

Stella nodded, a light replacing that question in her eyes. "I don't see any reason why we can't tell that to the children. I mean, it's like acting. You read what the scriptwriter puts on paper, you learn it, and then you act it out. I did that for twenty years."

Olivia wasn't so confident. "But I haven't."

"Posh!" Stella said. "I hadn't either when I started. And I didn't even go to acting school. I learned the hard way. Learned what it was like to feel rejected, alone, and criticized, and then acted it out on stage. You know those things. You can do it, too."

"You mean, we can just find something in the Bible, memorize what it says, teach it to the children, and have them act it out?"

"Sure. And it won't be like we're telling them something bad. We'll stick right by the script. Now what have I always told you?"

Nodding, Olivia felt a confidence that Stella often inspired in her. " 'All the world's a stage. . . .' "

"Exactly. Neil has to act in his job. He can't come right out and tell people their loved ones might be dying."

Seeing what she meant, Olivia could add to that. "I know Mama McCory and Hedda love cooking and serving the guests in the mornings. But sometimes Mama McCory's fingers are stiff and Hedda has a headache. But they act like everything is fine in front of the guests. So acting different than you feel isn't wrong, is it?"

"I don't think so. Remember that Sunday when Jacob

Whitfield preached on love? He said it's not a feeling, it's an action. So, he's saying to act it out."

"Like I'm acting like I love Neil."

"Yes. And he's acting like you're his wife."

That made it sound all right. "So it will be good for us to act like good Christians in church?"

"Exactly," Stella said. "That's what they all do. We're going to church like other people. The motto?"

"Life's a stage, and we play many parts." Olivia felt better. "By the time I finish my year here, I may not need acting school."

"And," Stella added, "the pastor said if people do acts of love, they may learn to love the ones they do the acts for."

Olivia nodded. "Proof of that is my pretending to be Mama McCory's granddaughter-in-law. I really love her now."

"So do I," Stella said.

Olivia wondered why she was staring at her and grinning. Then something occurred to her—something she refused to say aloud.

That kind of reasoning didn't extend to Neil, of course. She pushed a piece of popcorn in her mouth and chewed. Acting like she loved Neil wouldn't make her love him.

Except as her *employer*.

sixteen

At breakfast the next morning, Stella arranged for her and Olivia to go to Canaan Valley for her things. "I can get everything in the wagon that I need for winter."

"Don't you have appointments on Friday?" Hedda asked.

Olivia saw Mama McCory give her a strange look. Maybe she thought that was too personal, coming from Hedda.

"I mean," Hedda said, "maybe you get your hair done?"

"I do my own hair." Stella studied her for a moment. "Would you like for me to do something with yours?"

"No." Hedda turned away and busied herself in the kitchen.

"Now, I might," Mama McCory said. "I like that new short style. I might even have you give me a bob."

"I'll hold you to that. But as far as my appointment on Fridays," Stella said, loud enough for Hedda to hear, "I can't very well do that and live here, too."

Olivia wondered if her aunt would really be able to give up her job in the theater.

Their plans for the day were settled. Olivia and Stella would go to Canaan Valley and bring back Stella's belongings. Hedda and Bart would go up into Mama McCory's attic and bring down boxes of Christmas decorations.

While in Canaan Valley, Olivia sent a letter to her father.

Father,

I am very happy with my new job. It keeps me busy, so I will not be home for Christmas. Please tell John and Sarah "Merry Christmas" for me. Stella is doing well. She sends her love. I love you, too.

Olivia

Olivia and Stella decided to get the Christmas spirit going with dinner that evening. After Neil came home, he, Olivia, Stella, and Mama McCory ate at a table in the dining room in front of a fire blazing in the fireplace. Stella had made a centerpiece of lighted candles, evergreen sprigs, and a few Christmas baubles. Olivia had lit candles on other tables, lending a cozy, romantic feel to the room.

"Streun and I used to do this," Mama McCory said wistfully. "Just the two of us."

Olivia could imagine that. She glanced at Neil who also was looking at the setting and wondered if he was thinking he would like a romantic evening with someone special. It suddenly occurred to her that he couldn't pursue another woman even if he found one he cared about. In his mind, he was a married man.

After the blessing, Neil mentioned the Christmas decorations in the parlor. "I see *someone* is going to be hanging and stringing."

"After *someone* brings in several big trees," Stella quipped.

"Several?"

"Yes. This is a big house."

The women were all nodding. He sighed. "I see I'm outnumbered."

Judging by the way he smiled, Olivia thought he didn't mind at all.

"Thinking of Christmas," Olivia said, eager to hear their ideas, "what kind of children's program has the church had in the past?"

"The usual," Neil said. "Children act out the Christmas story."

"Um, which one?" Stella asked. "My goodness, I've been thinking of Charles Dickens's *A Christmas Carol*."

"I saw *A Christmas Carol* a long time ago," Mama McCory recalled. "It's a good story. But I don't think we have enough people in the church who can do that. Maybe you should keep it simple and just do the birth of Jesus."

"The birth of Jesus." Stella nodded. "You have a script for that?"

"Well, no. I don't think they've ever had a script. Jacob usually reads the story. The children wear their little costumes and act it out. Edith should have costumes from last year."

"I can show you where it is in the Bible," Neil offered.

"I just thought of something." Mama McCory nodded, remembering. "Edith said they lost their star."

"Oh, I'm so sorry," Stella said. "What happened?"

Mama McCory shrugged. "Probably got thrown in the trash."

Disbelief crossed Stella's face. "I've heard of an audience throwing rotten tomatoes at the star, but I wouldn't think church people would do that, much less throw somebody in the trash over a poor performance."

Mama McCory began to shake.

Neil put his napkin over his mouth. Then he moved it. "I'm sorry," he said, but he couldn't hold back a hearty laugh.

Mama McCory laughed aloud then.

"You were joking, of course," Stella said.

Mama McCory couldn't talk but nodded. Finally, she said, "I'm not talking about the star of the play. But—" She paused as she had trouble getting the words out. "I'm talking about the kind of star that hangs in the sky."

Neil couldn't keep a straight face.

"Oh. Ohh." Stella began to laugh, and so did Olivia.

Finally, wiping the tears from her face, Mama McCory said, "You just tickle me to pieces."

"The star of the Christmas show," Neil informed them, still emitting a few chuckles, "is the baby Jesus."

Stella was nodding. "That gives me something to go on. I don't know if I can do this the way you're used to."

Mama McCory gave her a straightforward look. "I don't think anybody really expects that."

Neil had come to realize that Juliet and Stella knew less about the Bible and Christianity than he had assumed. But they were eager to learn and take part. At least his grandmother was having the time of her life. He knew she loved Juliet and adored Stella.

The days of December flew by, and the inn constantly had children in it practicing for the play, women meeting for Bible study, and cooking going on in the kitchen. Neil did his part, too. He, Bart, Stella, and Juliet went out on the mountainsides until the right sizes and number of trees were found.

The big one in the foyer was twice as tall as he. A smaller one was placed in the corner on the stair landing. There was one in the dining room, one in the parlor, and a small one on the table in his grandmother's bedroom that would shine from her front window.

Each evening, he'd say, "Is that it?"

"Almost," Stella would reply. "But we do need this garland hung along the stair banister."

Another time, one of them would say, "We must have some of that holly with red berries," and then look at him as if the temperatures hadn't dropped to below freezing.

"Hot cocoa will be waiting when you return," Juliet said.

He jokingly complained but loved every minute of it, even when they sent him off to find mistletoe.

Another evening, he strung beads, then stood back watching the transformation while the three women added candles, silver wire ornaments, glass baubles, and tinsel to the big tree in the foyer.

They stepped back, looked at each other, and nodded.

"It still needs something else."

They began to murmur about what it could need.

"Stella," Neil said, pointing to the top of the tree. "That's the spot for you."

Her hands went to her hips. "What are you talking about?"

"That's where the star goes. You're the star of this decorating show, so go on up."

She rushed over and beat him on the arm. "Oh, you keep that up and you'll find yourself in the trash can."

His grandmother found her cardboard star outlined with silver tinsel. He hung it while the others lit the candles.

Instead of in a trash can, he found himself encased in a world of glowing candlelight, vivid colors, the smell of cedar, and three beautiful women who made him laugh, brightened his days, and gave him a family to come home to at night.

His gaze fell on Juliet, with her face lifted, staring at the tree as if she'd never seen anything so beautiful.

He hadn't. Not with the way the candles seemed to make a halo around her hair, her face, and her eyes. *Why, why*, he asked himself, *when a man has so much, must he always long for. . .more?*

&

A week before Christmas, they went to the church for the children's program. When Neil saw the cows on the stage when the curtain opened, he figured it would be entertaining but not too spiritual.

However, after the scene of no room at the inn and the young couple in the stable, the cows were led off the stage and outside.

The children's program was a huge success. Stella, Juliet, and the women and men they'd engaged to help had done a professional job of it. They'd even added a curtain that could be drawn across the stage. It had become a theater, and the children were in costumes befitting real shepherds and kings.

There was no forgetting of lines or giggling over children making mistakes. The program turned out to be meaningful, with the focus on the birth of Christ. The children took it very seriously and so did everyone in the audience.

Every child had a part, from the youngest real baby in the manger to the oldest. The oldest said the words "This is the

Savior of the world. This is Christ the Lord." The wonder of it came through.

Neil knew that Stella—this woman he suspected didn't know much about the Bible—was primarily responsible. Maybe it was her own wonder that caused it to come through in this performance. It was the old story presented in a fresh and awe-inspiring way.

The young actors questioned, "This baby is a king? Why is He born in a stable?" The participants asked more questions than they answered, causing the onlookers to think. "Why would God want us to bring these expensive gifts to this baby? Has anyone ever seen a star so bright? Why would an angel appear to us when we are just lowly shepherds?"

The musical ability of Stella and Juliet had to be what caused the children to sound like angels. Juliet played the piano, and Stella led them in her exuberant or quiet way, depending on the song.

At the end, Stella had everyone sing a hymn while leaving the church. The service had been solemn and worshipful. He reprimanded himself for having expected something rather outrageous to happen. All was quiet and peaceful.

All of a sudden, a loud crack disturbed his thoughts.

He and the pastor exchanged glances. They rushed to the door. Stella's wagon had been pulled up near the door. Bart and Carter stood in it, handing down paper bags.

Each one dipped into a bag, pulled out a Christmas cracker, and filled the night with pops, cracks, and laughter.

Neil took a bag and handed it to Juliet, then took his own. In it was an apple, an orange, nuts, a candy cane, pieces of hard candy, and a Christmas cracker. He and Juliet pulled the ends, popped theirs, and laughed. Their frosty breaths mingled in the cold December air and warmed his heart.

He spied his grandmother leaning against Stella for balance while she popped her cracker. She had refused to wear anything on her head, except the short haircut Stella had given her. It did look quite nice, but he feared she'd catch her death of cold. Soon she left with Stella in the wagon.

Neil and Juliet rode in the carriage. He tried to think of a way to express his gratitude. That weekly salary and ending their relationship in a year was becoming an albatross around his neck.

The stars were shining in the clear sky. The frosty air was invigorating, but not nearly so much as having this beautiful, talented, caring woman by his side. He'd warned himself not to say anything too personal. Maybe he could lead up to letting her know that her presence in his home—in his life—was far beyond any job offer he could imagine. Could she possibly be thinking along the same lines?

Finding his voice, he said, "I've never known the children's program to be so well done. I'm proud of you."

"Thank you. God gave us a beautiful story to work with." A touch of weariness seemed to have affected her voice.

"I suppose you're tired. You've worked so hard for this night."

"Oh, maybe a little," she said with a small smile. "But something is troubling me. Seeing the children and adults laughing and having so much fun on the church lawn tonight made me think of the children in the mining area. Just a paper bag with a few items in it would mean the world to them."

No, she hadn't been thinking of him. She was thinking of her unhappy childhood in the mining area. And after the wonderful reminder this night of what God had given the world, he should have been thinking of others, too.

"Should this be a church project?"

She nodded, and her smile lit up the night brighter than the soft moonlight that touched her face. He promptly turned the carriage around and drove to the pastor's house.

The Whitfields loved the idea, and by Tuesday morning the word had spread. The Bible study time turned into a time for goodies and toys being brought to the inn and bagged.

Neil came home for lunch to assist them, and in the evenings he helped some more. "I don't want to use only my money to buy toys and fruit," he said to Juliet. "I want to use my hands and heart in this project."

She nodded. "The pastor says it's more blessed to give than receive."

He smiled. All around him were happy faces. On Saturday he felt joyful when he and Juliet led the way up the mountain with a couple of wagons following.

Later, standing back and watching the miners' children excited about their gifts, parents looking on with happiness, and all laughing as they popped their Christmas crackers, he felt like he'd had an insight that had been missing.

He found fulfillment in being a doctor. Having watched his parents taken from him by the flu epidemic had enhanced his desire to help the sick. But that was also his profession. This—reaching out to the less fortunate—was not only a command of God, it was a heartwarming experience.

This wife of his was teaching him some important lessons. He couldn't remember a more meaningful Christmas.

❧

After the worship service on Christmas Day, Neil started a fire in the parlor and lit the candles on the Christmas tree. He, Juliet, his grandmother, and Stella were to exchange gifts. He couldn't imagine getting anything to bring him any more joy than he already had.

He was especially pleased to see his grandmother enjoying herself and looking so well. Even in the times she was not well enough to get out of bed, she always had someone, probably Hedda or Bart, get a gift for him. But while the gifts were always nice, he mostly just missed having her to celebrate with. He marveled that this year she was in the parlor acting as excited as a child, tearing paper from her gifts and exclaiming her delight and thanks.

They all were opening presents at one time like eager

children. Stella gave Mama McCory and Juliet headbands. Both promptly put them on. Neil slung a wool scarf around his neck and tried on a pair of gloves. Juliet draped a beautiful white-fringed shawl over his grandmother's shoulders.

He opened up the phonograph recordings Juliet got him, pleased that she must have remembered he'd commented how nice it was to have music in the house again.

She listened to the soft tinkling sound of the musical jewelry box he gave her. She liked it, but he didn't know how she would receive his other gift. Before she opened it, she exclaimed, "Oh, I only got you one gift."

"No," he said. "There are four recordings here."

She gave him that look. "It's only one gift."

"All right." He held out his hand. "Give it here."

She made a face and hugged it close. Then she began to tear off the paper and lifted the box lid. Her mouth opened in surprise. "Oh, you remembered."

Yes, he remembered the day she admired the black, jeweled purse in a shop window and wouldn't let him buy it for her.

While Stella and his grandmother admired it, Juliet looked at him with gratitude and said softly, "Thank you."

The gift that brought tears to her eyes, however, was the locket his grandmother gave her. "This is an heirloom," she said. "My and Streun's pictures were in here. Now it should have your and Neil's pictures."

Neil knew Juliet was touched by the gift. But he didn't know if the tears on her cheeks were because of the generosity of his grandmother or because she felt she had no right to accept it.

He wanted his expression to tell Juliet she had every right. But Juliet did not look directly at him again for a long, long time.

They all looked, however, when his grandmother handed him a legal document. "I don't want you to have to wait until I'm gone before you get this, Neil." It was the deed to the acres on the mountain where he'd often talked about building a house someday. The land he'd shown to Juliet in October—where he would like to someday settle down with his own family.

But it was not the gifts that touched his heart. In trying to make his grandmother's life more meaningful in her last months, he'd inadvertently done that for himself.

He would keep the memory of the togetherness, the caring, the reaching out to others—this Christmas—in his heart. . . forever.

seventeen

A big ice storm came at the end of January. That's when Carter came, almost frozen, saying a train had derailed going up a steep mountain curve from Canaan Valley to Sunrise. The injured were being taken to Sunrise Hospital. "It's bad," Carter said, shaking his head. "They need all the help they can get."

Olivia knew Neil hated to leave. Mama McCory had a bad cold she had been unable to shake. Even as he shrugged into his heavy coat, he gave instructions. "Make sure she gets her rest and takes her medication. When she's sick she won't always eat, but she needs to. And she needs plenty of water."

"We'll take good care of her," Stella promised.

He looked contrite. "I know you will. And"—he looked from one to the other—"take care of yourselves, too."

Without thinking, Olivia reached out and touched his sleeve. "You, too," she said softly. His gaze held hers for a long moment. He nodded, then pulled the hood up over his head and the gloves on his hands.

The ice and wind he went into were so cold that Olivia shuddered from having the door open only long enough for the doctors to leave. She turned, hugging her arms, and hurried to the parlor and stood in front of the fire. "Well," she said to Stella, "I guess it's just you and me."

"If anything happens to Mama. . ."

Olivia closed her eyes. "Don't even say it. I could never, never get over such a thing." She exhaled a deep breath. "Neil would never forgive us."

Stella put her arms around Olivia's shoulders. "You and I will become the best nurses ever." She brightened. "I played the part of a nurse one time."

Olivia hoped that would be good enough. "Let's go see our patient."

Keeping their patient in bed wasn't easy. By noon, Mama McCory was dressed and insisted on being up and around for lunch. "I was helpless for a long time," she said. "I don't mind resting, but I don't want to spend my life in bed if I don't have to."

"Fine," Stella said. "You stay in your room and read until lunch is ready."

Mama McCory agreed, with a look of triumph in her eyes.

"We can be as stubborn as she is," Stella growled. "She's not going to run around in this drafty house and blame us for getting worse."

They took the steaming chicken soup, slices of buttered bread made fresh that morning, and hot tea to the round table in front of her window. Olivia put another log in her fireplace. The three of them ate while looking out the window at the snow-covered ground. They agreed it looked beautiful but were concerned about the train wreck and wondered whether Neil was outside helping the injured or inside the hospital.

"I wish there was some way we could help," Olivia said, stacking their dishes after they'd eaten.

Suddenly, the sound of a horse's snort and whinny drew their attention to the window. Horses were struggling, pulling two creaking and groaning wagonloads of people up the long drive.

"Looks like your wish is about to come true," Mama McCory said. "This kind of thing happened several years ago, but there's no time to get into that now. We'd better get these people in before they freeze to death."

"You stay in this room," Stella demanded.

"Would you?" She answered her own question. "You'd be up and helping if you could. I know enough to take care of myself."

Olivia laid the coats in a pile as the six men, three women, and four children shucked them off and warmed themselves by the parlor fire. They told fearful tales of having to climb out of the leaning train car. Others had not been so fortunate.

"We were told the hotel and boardinghouse were full," one middle-aged man said. "We're grateful we can come here."

After they were warmed, Mama McCory sent men to get cots from the basement. "Others may come."

Before the day was out, there were eighteen. Some had injured loved ones in the hospital. Cots were set up in the dining room for the men. Women and children had the second floor.

Olivia felt she learned more about running an inn that day than in the months before. Although the travelers pitched in, she knew that making sure rooms were clean, making breakfast, and insuring they had a good food supply would be simple after having this crowd to care for.

Mama McCory said they wouldn't charge them for staying. "They aren't paying guests but stranded travelers. But if they offer something for the food, we can accept it."

That sparked an idea in Stella. She was already delighting everyone by adding different ingredients to the muffins, cakes, and candy she made. They played a game of guessing the ingredients.

After the first day, she wrapped her sweets in waxed paper, set them on a table in the dining room, and sold them. The guests called them "Stella's Sweets."

Men kept the fires going and even set up an unused bookshelf in the dining room for Stella's Sweets. They shoveled snow from the driveway all the way to the main road, then came in for the hot cocoa Olivia made.

Mama McCory warned that the electricity often went off in the wintertime. Some of the travelers responded they didn't even have electricity in their homes yet, so that wouldn't bother them. It stayed on, however. The travelers were able to make telephone calls, and by the end of the week, word came that trains could leave Sunrise again.

Some of the women were afraid. "It's the safest way this time of year," a man said. "That's why we have more railroad tracks than roads in these parts. Accidents happen. The good Lord took care of us and gave us a warm place to stay."

One of the women expressed what had gone through Olivia's mind. "Why do things like this have to happen?"

The man shrugged, looking troubled. "The engineer might have been going too fast, a rail could have been loose, something could have been on the tracks. . ."

"And, too," Mama McCory said, "if things like that never happened, you would never know how to appreciate it when they didn't."

The man smiled. "Now there's wisdom."

They all seemed to accept that, and by the end of the week they had all gone except one woman who stayed a couple of days longer until she learned her husband was well enough to travel.

The first evening after all the "guests" were gone, the inn seemed strangely quiet. Olivia and Stella were cleaning up from supper, and Mama McCory sat at the table with a cup of coffee. Olivia heard male voices coming from the foyer. She hadn't heard the knocker on the door or the bell on the desk.

She walked into the foyer to find a man with a coat draped around his shoulders. His left arm was in a splint and a sling. He held a travel bag with his right hand. A bearded man, who accompanied the man with the splint, was leaning over the desk, looking at the open ledger that was turned toward him.

"Sir?" she said forcefully at such impoliteness. "Can I help you?"

The bearded man straightened and faced her. His eyes looked tired, but they held a trace of mischief. "Yes, ma'am."

That's when she realized he was wearing Neil's coat. And he had Neil's voice.

"Oh, Neil." She rushed over to him and grabbed the sleeves of his coat. "I'm so glad you're all right." She looked up into his face. The mischief was gone from his eyes. He just looked tired. But his hand had come up and lay against her waist.

"It's good to be home," he said. "But I need a bath, a shave, and something to eat. We have a guest." He stepped back and introduced her to the man with him. "This is my wife, Juliet McCory."

That's when Olivia realized she had rushed to Neil as if having every right to be enveloped in an embrace from her husband who had been away. She had to ask him to repeat the man's name, then turned to the ledger and wrote, "Danny Quinn." "He may have the trillium room."

"I'll take him up."

But that was her job, and Neil looked unkempt and weary. "You need to get cleaned up, remember?"

"Don't nag, woman." He shucked off his coat and handed it to her.

Oh, so he wanted to play the husband-wife teasing game. She'd try it. "You're just like your grandmother. You never slow down."

"You're one to talk," he scoffed. "I heard about what went on here while I was gone." A dimple formed in Danny Quinn's cheek as he began to follow Neil up the stairs.

Later Neil walked into the kitchen, looking and smelling clean. That weariness was still in his face, however, and he looked thinner than he had a week ago. He hugged his grandmother and Stella. "Good to be home."

He'd invited Danny to supper, saying they both had eaten hospital meals all week. Danny seemed polite and nice. He was very muscular and looked to be around forty.

After the men had eaten their second bowlful of beef and vegetable stew and buttered bread, Olivia poured them another cup of coffee, and Stella brought over some of her wrapped sweets.

"I know you took all those people in and made them feel at home. I'm proud of you. But, Grandmother," Neil scolded, "I suppose you gave them your cold since you didn't follow the doctor's orders and stay in bed."

She shushed him. "I don't need a doctor to tell me when to get out of bed. Anyway, a lot of sickness is right up here." She tapped the side of her head. "Why, there's nothing like a houseful of people to invigorate me."

They all laughed. Olivia saw Stella nod. She'd told Olivia before that she drew energy from the crowds who watched her perform. That seemed to be how Mama McCory felt about having people around her.

Danny began to praise the sweet he was eating. "I've never tasted anything as good as this. Where'd it come from?"

That led to the discussion of Stella's Sweets. "You could make a fortune selling these." His grin at Stella dimpled his cheek and gave him a cute, boyish look.

That night after she and Stella were in bed, propped up with their now-usual bowl of popped corn, Olivia said, "I think Danny took a shine to you."

"Oh, I know his kind. He has those dark curls falling over his forehead and looks at you with those big blue eyes and gets those dimples in his face and expects a woman to fall for him. They probably have. But I'm not taken in. Anyway, I think he's too young for me."

"No, he's not. He has a lot of gray hair in those dark curls you noticed. I wonder what kind of work he does. . . ."

The next morning at breakfast they learned that Danny was a logger. "I can't do that kind of work with a broken arm," he told them.

"You need to be around where I can check that arm every day for at least another week," Neil told him. "It was a nasty break, and if you get infection in it, you could even lose it."

"To be honest with you, I don't have the kind of money to stay in a place like this. But I'll make it. Have all my life." He looked at Neil. "Don't suppose you could use some help around here?"

"What can you do?"

"Lot of things a man can do with one hand. I can carry logs and a coal scuttle, clean out a fireplace, and lay a fire. I can take care of horses and clean out a stable." He looked around at the women. "I reckon I can dust if I have to. And sweep. Even crack an egg with one hand."

Neil studied him for a while. "Room and board for a week in exchange for work. That is, if the ladies agree. They usually only serve breakfast to guests."

Olivia and Mama McCory looked at Stella, since she'd taken over most of the cooking. Danny's big soulful eyes pled with her.

"Oh, all right," Stella said. "Just know it's the egg-cracking part that swayed me."

Over the next few days, Danny proved to be a good worker. Having a man around during the day, even with only one good arm, was better than Olivia and Stella having to try and fix things themselves. The slats on an upstairs bed had fallen out. A curtain needed to be taken down so the hem could be sewn. There was always something.

Danny was fun, too, and since there were no guests in the inn and he was having meals with them, Neil invited him to join them in the parlor after their dinners.

Olivia enjoyed seeing how Neil related to another man. They seemed to go beyond the doctor-patient relationship to being friends. They discussed the bigger issues of progress and politics, but what she liked most was their banter over baseball teams and which were the better trout streams for fishing. Each claimed to have caught the bigger fish.

Some evenings, Olivia and Stella took turns playing the piano. Olivia played sheet music and hymns. Stella entertained them with her rambunctious style of playing. "Best not to sing the words to these," she'd say.

The icy wind howled outside, but they were warm and cozy by the fire, singing and laughing.

After several nights, Danny seemed unusually serious. He thanked them for taking him in like he was a part of a family.

"Don't you have any family?" Mama McCory asked.

"I've been on my own since I was sixteen. I roamed around, had odd jobs until I finally found a girl I wanted to settle down with." Danny paused as if to compose himself for what he was about to tell. "She went out on a boat one day. Something happened, and it capsized." He grimaced with the memory. "She couldn't swim, and nobody could get to her in time. She wasn't the only one that day. . . ." His voice trailed off, but he seemed to shake himself out of that mood. "So"—he slapped his knees—"I've been all over since—seeing the world, so to speak."

"What did you find was the most interesting?" Stella asked.

He looked at her a long time, curiously, as if she might be making fun, but she just stared back. Finally, he nodded. "The circus, I guess. I wanted to be the lion tamer, but the one who had the job kept his head, so I never did get to do that." Danny laughed lightly. "I did some trapeze work and even cleaned up after elephants. I'm experienced in a lot of things. I've also laid railroad tracks." He held up his hands. "Not the ones where the train derailed."

They laughed at that.

His serious mood returned as he said, "I have to leave tomorrow. There's business I have to take care of. You've all shown me what a real family should be like. I'll never forget it."

"You're welcome here anytime." Neil voiced what Olivia knew they all felt.

eighteen

Danny left the next morning after breakfast. His last words were, "I'll be back."

"He won't be back," Stella told Olivia when they were alone in the kitchen, cleaning up. "He's like many actors. They just can't stay in one place."

"You have for quite a while," Olivia said.

"It's all right for a man to travel around alone, but not for a woman when she gets a little age on her."

The house seemed cold, lifeless. There were no guests.

Olivia thought Neil missed Danny, too. They all obviously did, as it was much quieter during supper. They ate in the kitchen that was warm from the stove to avoid having to light fires in the dining room, making the house seem even colder.

After supper, Olivia expected they would all turn in early. Neil had enjoyed a male friend. He probably preferred that over having to pay attention to his "wife." She expected Neil would have her play something and probably suggest they all turn in early.

They did go to the parlor as usual after supper. Neil threw on another log, and soon the glow and warmth of the fire displaced the former chill of the room. Mama McCory settled on the couch with her embroidery.

When Neil went to the phonograph, Olivia thought he knew none of them felt like being too lively tonight. She saw him look through the recordings, then one she gave him for Christmas began to fill the room with the melodic tones of "Sweet Adeline."

Neil walked over to where she stood near the fire. "Shall we try our hand at a game of checkers?" he said, as if that were a usual night's event. It wasn't, of course.

Olivia nodded. She hadn't played in a long time.

He took first the checkerboard table then the two straight chairs away from the window and brought them closer to the fire and the couch, then sat.

Olivia looked at Mama McCory and Stella. They lifted their eyebrows and shrugged.

Neil opened the drawer in the checkerboard table. "Black or red?"

"Red." She sat and scooted up to the table.

He filled her side of the board with red, then started on his side with black. "On your mark, get set—"

"Are we running a race or playing checkers?"

"The goal is to win, fast or slow." He set down the last black checker with a sense of finality and moved closer to the table.

Olivia could hardly believe the challenge in his dark eyes. All right, so he played to win. Well, he would find out his meek and mild wife could be just as determined. She made her first move.

Before long, accompanied by "In the Shade of the Old Apple Tree," Neil leaned back and rubbed his hands together in victory.

"That was your lucky win."

"Two out of three, then."

He won the next one and wore a triumphant grin while placing the checkers.

"I need some hot chocolate," Olivia said. What she needed was to get her wits about her. She'd expected Neil to be sad that his new friend had left. Instead, he was acting like he wanted nothing more than an evening with his "wife" and family.

As they continued to play several games, he even joined in softly singing, "Ida, Sweet as Apple Cider."

Olivia stared at the board as if trying to figure out a move. Much of the time, however, she marveled at how sincere Stella sounded about embroidery. One would think she was simply a middle-aged mother enjoying a quiet evening.

"My mother taught me when I was a girl," Stella said. "But I haven't done this in years."

"Stella Kevay," Mama McCory scolded, "I know you heard Neil tell me to take up embroidery again because the exercise might be good for my fingers. Now you've become his nurse, making me use my hands."

Stella didn't deny it. "Sounds like a good reason to me."

The wood popped and crackled in the fireplace. Olivia felt the warmth and smelled the wood smoke mingled with hot chocolate when she lifted the cup to her lips. At least she did not smell that faint musky fragrance.

She could not sit there and think all night, so she made a move on the checkerboard and to her surprise was able to jump several of Neil's black men. "Crown me," she said.

He did. Finally, he was cornered. "You win," he said and sat back with his thumbs hooked into the armholes of his vest. He seemed pleased.

"It's about time," she said.

"All you needed was a good teacher. You've watched me win several times tonight, and you're finally getting the hang of it."

She scoffed. "Oh, so you're taking credit for my win."

"Of course."

Olivia shook her head and went over to look at the little bluebirds with pink ribbons in their beaks that the two women were embroidering on pillowcases. Soon, however, Mama McCory said she must turn in. "You know the saying that 'early to bed and early to rise makes one healthy, wealthy, and wise.'"

"I should try it," Stella said.

"Oh, but you must be very wise, having come from the mining area, raising your daughter alone, and even sending her to college. That must have been a great sacrifice for you."

"When Juliet went to college, she lived with my brother in the city. He paid for her education."

Olivia was glad Stella had not lied about that. She simply omitted the fact that her brother was also Olivia's father.

"That's good." Mama McCory was nodding. "Families should help out. That's what I've told Neil when he has said I've sacrificed for him. Trying to be a parent to Neil was never a burden. Oh, he could be a pistol at times, but it's still a joy to care for someone you love."

Olivia watched warmth come into Neil's eyes when he looked at his grandmother and smiled. They all seemed rather mesmerized as "By the Light of the Silvery Moon" permeated the room.

Then the music stopped.

Olivia realized she was toying with the locket Mama McCory had given her for Christmas. She often wore it, although there were no pictures of her and Neil inside. The locket was empty. She quickly moved her hand from the locket and with her glance saw the rings she wore.

It wasn't often she thought about it. But someday she'd take off the locket for the last time. She had no right to Mama McCory's locket, Neil's mother's engagement ring, or Neil's wedding band. Did he ever think of that?

He got up and put the screen close around the fireplace. There would be ashes by morning. Just like the warmth of this room, the laughter, the togetherness, the love. . .someday, those things, too, would be ashes.

nineteen

March winds whistled through the trees. Much of the landscape remained blanketed with snow and ice until the rains and floods of April washed them away. First came the white dogwood and yellow forsythia. Then tender red maple buds and tender green leaves made their appearance.

So did Danny.

His arm had healed and was getting stronger every day. Neil gave him a job and also the room on the lower floor that Bart and Hedda had in the summers when they stayed overnight at the inn.

Sunshine and longer days meant Danny would be painting or repairing until late. He still had time to comment on Stella's Sweets. "You could sell these all over."

"Fine," she huffed. "You get the stores to buy them, and I'll bake them."

So he did. Before long, he was acting as her promoter, selling her sweets to the general store, the Soda Shoppe, the bakery, the grocery store, and even the bakeries and shops down in Canaan Valley. He'd found out how to get paper with Stella's Sweets printed on it. Before long, he had her baking and packaging, and he sent her sweets on the train to the nearby cities.

Danny wasn't just a friend anymore, he was a full-time employee. *Like I am*, Olivia often thought. She and Stella, and even Mama McCory, spent time in the evenings in the flower beds making sure the inn would be spectacular for tourist season.

Danny began sitting beside Stella on the family pew at church. On Easter Sunday, Pastor Whitfield talked about

Jesus, who grew to be a man and was sacrificed for everyone in the world who would believe in Him.

He said now that the mountains had thawed, new people would be moving in, so they needed to spread the gospel. And they could now baptize people in the river.

Later, when they were changing out of their Easter bonnets and fancy clothes, Stella asked Olivia, "You think we should get dipped in the river?"

"Do you understand all that? I mean, what they mean about Jesus coming into your heart?"

"I think it's a symbol, like baptism. The church members didn't have some kind of heart attack. It's ridiculous to think this little Man, or big Man, climbs in there and lives."

"That sounds funny," Olivia said. "But I'm not about to laugh. God might think I'm making fun of Him."

"I know," Stella said seriously. "I'm just trying to figure all this out, too. But if we're going to do this right, we have to do what the other church members do and learn to be good Christians."

Olivia sighed. "I keep hearing that we're supposed to have Jesus in our hearts, but nobody tells us how to do that."

Stella agreed. "We need to ask without sounding completely ignorant."

That evening when they, Neil, and Mama McCory had a light supper in the kitchen, Olivia approached the subject she and Stella had discussed. "Baptism," she began. "The church I went to in Davidson never mentioned it. But, um, Pastor Whitfield talked about being baptized in the river."

"Different churches have different symbols for showing a change has taken place inside someone," Neil said. "Pastor Whitfield likes to take believers down to the river and baptize them."

"I've heard of that," Stella said. "You mean he holds them underwater?"

Neil saw his grandmother put her hand to her mouth, and

she chuckled. "Not hold them under," Neil said. "He just takes them under until they're covered with water, then brings them up. That symbolizes being dead to the old self and starting a new life living according to the teachings of Jesus."

"So, since Stella and I go to church and we are having the Bible studies again, should we be baptized? Otherwise, are we being hypocrites?"

Olivia didn't know what the ensuing silence meant. When her gaze met Mama McCory's, the woman said, "I'm thinking on this." She looked at her grandson. "Neil?"

Finally, Neil said, "You may be right. If the church people knew you hadn't been baptized, they might think you don't believe like we do. But," he said quickly, "baptism doesn't save you. It's a symbol of what you believe."

"Save?" Stella said. "From what?"

"From being eternally separated from God after you die."

"Oh-wee," Stella said forcefully. "Now there's a tragedy." Recovering, she gave a thin smile. "Would you explain what your church members believe about all that? I mean," she added quickly when a surprised look came onto Neil's face, "in case it's different from some other churches. We've had to move around so much, it's hard to remember it all."

Neil's eyes looked stuck on Stella.

Olivia's quick glance at Mama McCory revealed she must still be thinking. Her lips were clamped together, and she stared at her iced tea glass. Without looking up, she said, "All you have to do is believe in Jesus."

"That's true, Grandmother," Neil said. "But there's more to it. You do believe in Jesus, don't you?"

"Well, of course." Stella sounded insulted. "There has never been a time when I didn't believe in Jesus and whatever the Bible says."

Neil must have detected indignation. "I think," Neil finally said, "we should have Pastor Whitfield talk to you about what our church believes."

The following week, Danny walked down to the front of the church to ask Jesus into his heart, and they all went down to the river to see him and some others baptized.

"What's Danny's going to think about me," Stella said, "when he finds out I'm just pretending to be a good Christian?"

Olivia felt bad about it, too. "Maybe Neil is right. We need to talk to the preacher."

In May, when spring was alive in all its glory, workers returned to their work of building shops and homes. Roads were being built or improved.

Tourists arrived on the trains. Business at the inn was booming, along with Stella's Sweets. There was no time for special talks, with the preacher or anybody.

twenty

Neil had an emergency and couldn't get away from the clinic in time for his grandmother's birthday party. When he arrived home after 3:30, he met the Whitfields, Mary and Janie Clayton, and some of the church women leaving in their carriages.

At least he got to greet Bart when he rode up to the stable and Danny took Sally's reins. "Those women of yours sure know how to have a good time," Danny said. Bart agreed and laughed.

Walking up to the house, Neil thought with pleasure how much he appreciated Juliet and Stella suggesting this party. These past months of activity had enlivened his grandmother. But hanging over their heads was still the specialists' diagnosis of her failing heart. This might be the last party she would ever have.

He walked right up to his grandmother who sat at one of the dining room tables with gifts in front of her. He sat beside her and handed her a book by her favorite author, Grace Livingston Hill.

"Oh, *The Finding of Jasper Holt*. I don't have that one." She kissed his cheek.

He was glad to see Hedda again. She, along with Juliet and Stella, slipped on their aprons and began to clean up from the party.

"I'll get you some tea and cake," Stella said.

Before she could, however, rushed footfalls sounded from someone coming into the inn from the main entrance. A middle-aged, well-dressed man appeared, his face scrunched like he was in pain.

Neil's first thought was that the man had been hurt. But that didn't make sense. Surely he would have gone to the hospital or clinic.

Neil stood when the man stepped farther inside the room, looking past him and around the room. He hadn't noticed the woman with the man until she stepped up and pulled on the man's arm, which he shrugged away.

Suddenly the man, in a booming voice, ground out, "So this is the kind of job you took? A waitress?"

Juliet squealed. She dropped a tray of dirty dishes, and it crashed onto the hardwood floor. Small china teacups broke. Stella rushed over and put her arms protectively around Juliet's shoulders.

The man glared at Stella. "I should have known the two of you would be in this together." With two long steps, he reached Juliet and took hold of her arm at the same time Neil reached him.

Neil grasped the man's arm. "Get your hands off her."

The man sneered. "I'll do as I please with my daughter."

Tightening his hold on the man's arm, Neil raised his right hand and circled the man's throat. "You will not do as you please with my wife. I'm a doctor. My fingers are on the pressure points that can have you on that floor before you can blink an eye."

Neil surprised himself with the intensity of his emotions. But he didn't back down. "And sir, that's the nice part of what I can do to you."

The man let go of Juliet. "I'm her father." He sounded like a man with a sore throat.

"I'm her husband." Neil glared at him. "Shall we sit down and discuss this like. . .civilized men?"

The man nodded. Neil looked at Juliet.

"It's all right," Juliet said in a small voice.

Her stark face and the fearful look in her eyes indicated everything was not all right. But Neil moved his hands away, still watching the man as he straightened his collar and tie.

"Now why don't you 'civilized' men sit down?" Stella said. "All you need is some tea. Everyone just calm down until I bring it." She looked around, smiling. "Would anyone like a tea cake?"

"No," Neil and the man ground out at the same time.

The woman with him said, "Yes, thank you. That would be nice." She put her arm through the man's. That's when her appearance registered. She looked to be around fifty, with a lot of gray in her hair that was pulled back in a neat roll. She looked pleasant and refined in a conservative dress and jacket.

Neil gestured toward the clean table next to the one where his grandmother sat. He was afraid such a confrontation might upset her, but her coloring looked good and her breathing seemed fine. In fact, she smiled as if enjoying the scene.

"Yes," Mama McCory said, "please, have a seat." She moved her chair around to see them better.

The pleasant woman stepped over to the table and turned her head toward the irate man. He exhaled heavily, then pulled out the chair for her. She thanked him. He sat in a chair next to her.

Hedda had picked up the dirty and broken dishes. "I'll be glad to serve the tea."

Stella took the seat next to the pleasant woman. Neil held out a chair and nodded for Juliet to sit next to Stella. He would be between Juliet and the man in case he needed to protect her.

"This is a nice place," the woman said, as if she had just dropped in on a friend for a cup of tea. "I've heard about it and have seen it advertised as one of the lovelier places to visit in Sunrise. But this is my first time here."

While Hedda served the tea, Stella agreed that it was a lovely place and spoke of travelers and tourists who made reservations to return at the same time each year.

Neil wondered how Stella could be so cordial to this woman. If this man was Juliet's father, like he said, wouldn't he be Stella's husband? But he was here with another woman. And Juliet's father was supposed to be a poor miner, wasn't he? This man's appearance was more like that of a prosperous businessman.

Stella stared at Hedda, who seemed to be taking an incredibly long time pouring the tea and bringing a tea cake to the woman. "Thank you," Stella said, and soon Hedda left the dining room.

"Now," Stella said in a commanding voice. "I'm probably the best one to explain everything since the men are acting like children competing for the last cookie in the jar."

The man made a sound like a growl deep in his throat. Neil glanced at him quickly. The man sighed and leaned forward with his forearms on the table as if resigned to some dastardly fate.

"It's simple." Stella lifted her hands. "She met and married Dr. Neil McCory." She pointed at Neil. "Married him last September." Her voice lowered. "Herman, she knew you would object, so she was afraid to tell you."

Neil watched the man's mouth move, from closed to open, closed to open. Finally, he said, "That's all I ever wanted for her—to settle down and marry someone and live like normal people."

"Well, I did," Juliet said.

The man sat back, seeming to relax. His eyes swept over the room and back again. "Then you're not working as a waitress?"

"Not that anything's wrong with that," Stella said with spirit. "I'll bet you've been served by many of them and enjoyed the meal."

A tinge of color came into the man's cheeks, as if he'd felt the brunt of her reprimand.

"But for your information," Stella continued, "she manages this inn. After all, she is the wife of Dr. McCory, which makes her the granddaughter-in-law of Mrs. McCory, who owns this place." Stella held out her hand toward Mama McCory, as if presenting her.

The man acknowledged Neil's grandmother with a polite nod. He seemed at a loss for words. Finally, he said, "This inn does have a fine reputation." He took a deep breath and exhaled. "And so do Stella's Sweets."

"This is delicious," said the woman eating the small cake. "I had one at the Canaan Valley bakery."

"That's how we found you," the man said. "I've sent letters that were never answered. I inquired at the post office and was told your mail had been picked up. I even visited your cabin after the weather cleared up. The baker said Stella's Sweets came from Sunrise."

"At the first store we stopped in," the woman said, "they knew who you were and said Herman could find you here."

The man looked smug. "So here we are."

"One big, happy family." Stella gave him a stony look.

He returned it, then snapped, "I don't know what you're doing, Stella." He looked at Juliet. "But I'm glad to see you're behaving responsibly."

Neil didn't care for the man's tone. "Please speak politely to the ladies, Mr. Kevay."

"The name's Easton."

Bewildered, Neil tried to make sense of it. He figured Stella and Mr. Easton must have divorced and then Stella married a Mr. Kevay, who adopted Juliet.

But this man's attitude wasn't like one who had given up rights to his daughter. The only Easton he'd ever heard of was the name of the coal that ran daily from the mining area to other parts of West Virginia.

The man spoke again, more politely this time. "Olivia, I'm pleased that you gave up that wild dream of yours and that you're married. I've worried about you and wanted to know that you were all right. And another reason I wanted to find you"—he touched the shoulder of the woman next to him—"I want you to meet the woman I'm going to marry."

Neil nodded at the woman Mr. Easton introduced as Evelyn James. But he was thinking about the man calling Juliet "Olivia."

Stella had told them that Juliet had lived with her brother in the city when she went to college. So this was Stella's brother? But he said he was Juliet's father. Had she called him her father when she had lived with him? He'd apparently cared about her, having her live with him while she attended college.

"Maybe I was too hard on you," Mr. Easton said to Juliet. He smiled with a more tender look than Neil expected. "Evelyn has pointed out some errors of my ways. She's a fine lady whose deceased husband was pastor of a church in Thurmond. She moved to Davidson after he died."

"I'm happy for you," Juliet said.

Mr. Easton spoke almost contritely. "I met her through friends but never thought we'd have anything in common. I soon discovered we didn't. But her faith, charity, and sweet spirit intrigued me. She's softened my heart in many ways." He took a deep breath. "You're my sister, Stella. I've been rough on you. I'm sorry. I do love you and hope you can forgive me."

The next thing Neil knew, Juliet, Stella, and Mr. Easton were standing and hugging, with tears in their eyes.

So this man was not Stella's ex-husband. He was her brother. Was Juliet's middle name, or first name, Olivia? Had Juliet and Stella decided to use a name different from what Mr. Easton had called her so they could stay hidden from him?

Now Mr. Easton was inviting them all to his wedding at his home in Davidson. Evelyn gave details and smiled at Juliet. "I would be so pleased if you would be my matron of honor."

Neil couldn't figure it all out. He stared at his cup of tea, cold now. Juliet, whom he would like to be his wife permanently, was the one to make explanations.

She was his wife, yes. . .but only for another two months. And she wasn't obligated to tell him anything.

That was not in the contract.

❧

Olivia walked to the side window, watching as her father and Evelyn rode out of sight. She tried to concentrate on the trees outside, lush and green in the sunshine. The scenery became blurry, however, and there wasn't even any rain.

She wasn't sure what Neil and Mama McCory were thinking, but she could guess some of it. All she did know was that her father had said his name was "Easton" and he had called her "Olivia." What could she say?

Suddenly, she realized she couldn't tell Mama McCory anything. She was here in a binding contract with Dr. Neil McCory—her employer. She could offer no explanation to Mama McCory without his permission.

She was not even his legal wife, contrary to what he thought. She was nothing more than a hired hand, making a weekly salary.

"Juliet," Mama McCory called.

Olivia swiped at her eyes and turned. Neil and Stella had done the same, with concerned looks on their faces.

"Thank you all so much for the party. It's the nicest, most fun one I've ever had." Mama McCory smiled. "And you certainly surprised me."

Olivia held her breath. Did she mean she was surprised that somebody had apparently not been truthful with her? She'd been gracious in saying she was glad to meet Olivia's father and Evelyn. Was now the time for questions?

"It's been a long, interesting day," she said. "But I'd like to rest for a while."

Olivia waited for the next words. What would they be?

"If somebody would take my gifts to the parlor, we can all look at them after supper." Mama McCory grinned. "And you two girls will have to sing and dance that birthday song for

Neil. He missed it. Hedda," she called, and Hedda stepped into the dining room.

Olivia suspected Hedda had been near enough to hear everything from the time the tray crashed to the floor and the dishes broke.

Mama McCory told Hedda, "I appreciate all of your help today." The two women hugged.

"Are you...all right?" Hedda asked her.

"Never better," Mama McCory said.

Hedda looked as if she'd like to say something else, but Mama McCory turned to leave the room. Hedda then left the room herself.

Right after Hedda left, Neil took a deep breath, then exhaled. "I need to check Grandmother's vital signs." He followed Mama McCory to her room.

Without bothering with the dishes, Olivia and Stella went to their bedroom and propped up on the bed.

"That was quite a family reunion in the dining room," Stella said wryly. "You and I have finally gained Herman's approval."

Feeling helpless, Olivia sighed. "Think how mad he'll be when he learns the truth. He will never want to see me again."

Stella agreed. "He will blame me for this. I guess I am to blame. He always said actors were rogues and vagrants. Maybe I've proved that's true." Stella's face clouded. "Not in being an actor, but in what I've done to you."

"What you've done to me, Stella," Olivia said, "is given me the chance to save money for acting school. A chance to see what a real, loving family can be like. And a chance to grow up. I think I was a headstrong, rebellious girl. But so much has happened here. I've learned to care about other people instead of just what I want."

"I know what you mean. I've found a kind of meaning like I've never known when caring for Mama McCory, the inn, Stella's Sweets, the Bible studies, and...even Danny."

"Oh, Stella, I know he's crazy about you."

"He won't be when he finds out what I've done. He thinks all this is legitimate and that I'm your mother. He thinks we're a family—the kind he never had but would like to have." She sighed. "I've really messed up this time."

There seemed to be no solution. Then Olivia remembered something. "Do you suppose this is one of those times when forgiveness comes into play? Pastor Whitfield preached about it. If we tell the truth and ask forgiveness, wouldn't Mama McCory and Neil forgive us? They are good Christians, you know."

A sad expression crossed Stella's face. "Not if the truth causes Mama McCory to have another stroke."

twenty-one

The inn was filled for the next couple of weeks with tourists and vacationers coming to the mountains to escape the heat of the cities. Neil was busy, too, since a lot of his patients couldn't come down the mountain during the winter and had their checkups in the summer. He deliberately made more visits to the hospital and house calls. He stayed later than necessary at the clinic, thinking and praying.

This was a busy time for Juliet and Stella, but he had the feeling they were as tense as he. His grandmother, who usually picked up on everything, didn't seem to notice that anything was different. Maybe her stroke had affected her brain. Or maybe she was ripe for another one.

Finally, Neil had to scoff at himself. He'd wanted to make the last months of his grandmother's life a happy time. He'd hired someone to do that, and that someone was doing her job well. He's the one who was failing to contribute to his grandmother's quality of life.

Was it really his business whether Mr. Easton was Juliet's father? Or her uncle? Stella's ex-husband? Or her brother?

Or if Juliet was Olivia? Or both? Or. . .neither?

He slammed his fists down on his desk in the clinic. Then, rubbing the sides of his hands, wondering if he'd broken a couple of bones, Neil berated himself. He had no right to harbor this attitude of having been betrayed by Juliet.

She owed him nothing. He owed her everything.

His actions should not be dependent upon what another person was or wasn't. Only what he, himself, was.

That evening he told Juliet he would accompany her to the wedding.

"I'll stay here," Stella said. "And I'll send Danny to ask Hedda to help out."

❧

"Are you worried about seeing Mr. Easton again?" he asked when they were on the train Friday morning, headed for Davidson. Both he and Juliet had hardly spoken to each other during the past two weeks, except for casual conversation.

"No," she said. "I'm worried about what you think."

"I have no right to think anything." Immediately, he thought that might sound like she was nothing more than his employee. He looked over at her, so lovely in her tailored suit and pert little hat.

"Juliet," he began, wanting to explain, "I want to know all about you. Since we married, I've found out enough about you to know that you're a fine person. You're beautiful, you're kind, you're—"

"No," she stopped him. "I'm none of those things. I don't know if I can even tell you the truth about me."

"Whenever you're ready to confide in me, Juliet," he said, "I want to listen."

She nodded, and he thought she wiped a tear from her eye before she turned to look out the window where trees were less dense and flatter land appeared.

He'd called ahead so Mr. Easton would know when to expect them. What he didn't expect was to be met by a driver in a roadster who took their bags and put them into the automobile.

Neil climbed in after Juliet, grateful the three of them could fit in the two-seater. She pointed out various places as they traveled the roads and eventually along Main Street. He was somewhat familiar with Davidson. However, he had not been in this part of town.

When the driver pulled up in front of the impressive palatial house, Neil got a strange feeling he should have worn a more formal suit. This didn't fit the picture of a poor girl from a mining town. But it did fit the picture of a young woman whose uncle, or father, would pay her expenses to college. . .at least.

A housekeeper opened the door and addressed Juliet as "Miss Easton." Neil was welcomed warmly by Mr. Easton and met John and Sarah Easton, who were introduced as "Olivia's" brother and his wife.

When Mr. Easton said Mrs. Cooper would show them their room, Neil felt a moment of panic. How could he not have expected that? Now he supposed his bed that night would be a chair.

Juliet spoke up, however. "Oh, I was wondering if Sarah and I might share a room tonight. We've never spent much time together."

"Well, I was an old married woman when you were still a schoolgirl. It's about time we got together for some girl talk. And we have a lot to talk about." Her rather plain face took on a glow. "I have to tell it."

Having seen women patients act like that before, Neil had a good idea what she had to tell.

"I'm in the family way. We were beginning to think it would never happen."

Juliet reached out, and they hugged each other. "I'm going to be an aunt," Juliet said. "Yes, we have a lot to talk about."

During dinner, where Juliet was being served rather than serving others, what Neil suspected was confirmed. Herman Easton owned several mines and lumber mills. He was not surprised to learn that John, in his pleasant but formal manner and wearing eyeglasses, was an accountant for his father's businesses. Sarah taught piano lessons in her home.

Neil felt they were interested in and appreciated his medical practice in Sunrise. He was impressed anew with how articulate Juliet was about her responsibilities at the inn. Her enthusiastic rendering of her activities—learning to cook, playing piano at church, having Bible studies—seemed to impress them. Her sincere love for Stella and his grandmother was evident.

Mr. Easton seemed pleased. "I'm glad to hear that you and Stella have settled down and you got that foolishness out of your system."

Foolishness? Neil wondered what that foolishness was. Why had Juliet and Stella led him to believe they had been victims of abuse or poverty? He realized he had assumed many things that had not been explicitly stated. Just what was going on with this "wife" of his?

Neil didn't have an opportunity to question her about that, even if he had the right. After dinner they discussed the wedding, and Sarah played the music she would play the following day. John and Sarah had traveled a good portion of the day, so they wanted to retire early. They all decided to turn in early.

Midmorning on Saturday, they all took their places in the parlor, not larger but more luxurious than the one at Sunrise Inn. Neil sat on a couch with the pastor's wife, Evelyn James's sister, and her brother-in-law. The pastor stood in front of the fireplace that was hidden by pots of white flowers and a mantel decorated with white flowers and lighted candles. John stood on one side of the pastor beside Mr. Easton.

But Neil's eyes were only on Juliet. She looked so lovely in a soft blue dress, with her hair hanging below her shoulders, quite different than on the day they were married. She looked like she belonged here, not in that small cabin wearing an unimpressive dress.

Sarah began to play "The Wedding March," and Neil stood with the others as Evelyn walked in, wearing an ivory-colored lace gown. She kept looking at Mr. Easton with love-filled eyes. Juliet hadn't looked at him when they married.

Juliet held the orchid bouquet while Herman Easton slipped a ring on Evelyn's finger. In his wedding to Juliet, the bouquet had been smelly marigolds.

Who was that stranger standing there? Was she really his

wife? The family relationship and background didn't match with what she and Stella had led him to believe.

Were they married or did she lie?

Why had she wanted the. . .job?

Was it all some kind of foolishness?

❧

A trip to the coast followed by their returning to West Virginia to see the sights of the state together is something Neil would liked to have done with Juliet. However, that was the trip planned by the newlyweds, Herman and Evelyn Easton.

Since their annulment was to take place in September, Neil had thought the ideal time would be in August. He had imagined standing above Blackwater Falls as it fell over rocks as high as a five-story building. Then he and Juliet would go deep into the earth and explore the caverns. The best place he would take Juliet would be to see the spectacular shower of stars. He would tell her she lit up his life like that and ask if they could make the marriage permanent.

Now, however, after the Eastons left on their honeymoon and John and Sarah left to return home, he and Juliet had nothing to say. Their train would leave in the afternoon. It seemed they had reverted, not as far back as to the day they first met, but to the second day, when each was so careful and uncertain about what to say or do.

That was decided for them when the telephone rang. Juliet picked up the receiver immediately. "Yes, this is she. Stella, what's wrong?"

She went so pale, Neil thought she might faint. But if Stella was making the phone call and something was wrong, he knew what it had to be.

Juliet didn't seem able to speak. Her eyes turned to him, and he saw her fear.

He took the phone from her. "Neil here. What is it, Stella?" He closed his eyes as he repeated what he thought she said.

"Grandmother's in the hospital?" He listened to the skimpy details. Stella was usually in control of every situation. Now she sounded panicked. He knew this had to be bad. "I'll be there as soon as possible."

I? Neil realized he didn't say, "We."

Would this. . .Juliet Olivia Kevay Easton McCory. . . return with him?

She was a city girl; he saw that now. She'd done something that had displeased her father, uncle, foster parent, whomever, but the man had forgiven her and they were on good terms again.

He turned to her. "Grandmother's in the hospital."

She was shaking all over. "What happened?"

How many times had he asked that question of patients or someone who brought them into the clinic? There was always a story behind a fact. But he didn't know this one. He could only say, "She fell."

Juliet turned away. "I'll get my things."

Yes, she planned to return with him. After all, she was under contract—with the job—for another two months.

They all had been quieter at home—going through the motions, ignoring the tension—over the past two weeks since Mr. Easton came and called "Olivia" his daughter. Looking back, he could see that might well be the beginning of his grandmother's stroke, if that's what caused her to fall. His grandmother was smart enough to know the implications of that day. If Juliet was Olivia Easton, what did that mean?

After many miles of thinking and hearing the *chug-chug* of the train winding around the mountains, going higher, the forest becoming denser, he felt his mind became like the forest. The miles of thinking brought no answers.

Juliet looked miserable. But why? Was she like Kathleen, deciding she preferred city life now that she and Mr. Easton were on good terms? He could ask *something*. Whether she answered would be her choice.

"Juliet," he said, "who are you?"

"Olivia Easton."

"Not. . .Juliet Kevay?"

She shook her head.

Olivia Easton played on his mind with the sound and rhythm of the wheels on the track. . .going, going. *If she's not Juliet Kevay, then she's not Mrs. Neil McCory.*

She didn't move. He watched her profile as she stared out the window, seeing. . .what? "Were you mistreated at. . ." He didn't even know what the relationship really was. Was Herman Easton her father? Uncle? Foster parent? What? He tried again. "At the Easton home?"

He thought she wouldn't answer.

Finally, her stark face turned toward him, but she didn't raise her eyes to his. "I thought I was."

He strained to hear her words.

"As far back as I can remember, I wanted to be an actress. Father refused to support me if I pursued that. I took this. . . job to save money so I could go to acting school in New York this fall."

He had told her at the beginning that he wanted her to pretend for his grandmother's sake. Was their entire relationship a pretense on her part? He'd begun to believe she cared for him. Maybe because that's what he wanted to believe. They seemed right for each other.

Now he knew it was all an act. An act that he had begun to believe. Soon the curtain would close. Many times he'd thought of her name that represented one of the great love stories of all times. Now he realized just how fitting it was.

Shakespeare's *Romeo and Juliet* ended in tragedy.

twenty-two

The prognosis was inconclusive. The only thing the specialists seemed to know for sure was that Mama McCory had extensive bruising and a couple of cracked ribs from the fall.

Neil could have told them that.

What he did know was that she looked helpless and frail, her face and hair as white as the sheets on which she lay. He knew the doctors were keeping her heavily sedated. She would moan sometimes from the pain of even a shallow breath but never open her eyes. Neil feared she might never do that again. Pneumonia was also a concern, and she was allowed no visitors.

After several days, the specialists were still trying to determine if a heart attack or stroke caused the fall. They needed more tests. Neil felt they were not as open as they had been when she had her stroke and they discovered her weak heart. He feared the worst.

When the doctors said they would be consulting with another specialist, Neil could only nod. Here he was a doctor but helpless to do anything for his own grandmother except pray and wonder what they were doing in her room so much of the time.

Carter assured him he was taking care of the patients at the clinic. Neil visited his patients in the hospital and sat in the waiting room—not as a doctor but as a helpless person concerned about a loved one in the hospital. He wasn't allowed to stay in her room at night, so he slept in an empty room with the promise he'd be called if any change took place.

On one of the rare times when they weren't poking, prodding, testing, or consulting, Neil sat by her bedside, held her cold, thin hand in his, and confessed that he had deceived her. His intentions were good and the results had been good, but he had not been completely honest with her. Although she couldn't hear him, he asked her forgiveness.

Finally, he was told she could have regular visitors. Her pain medication had been lessened and she was lucid at times, but most of the time she slept.

"Her breathing is not as painful now that her ribs are healing," one specialist said with a reassuring smile.

Neil wasn't reassured. Why did they keep talking about ribs? They should be more concerned about the bigger issues of stroke and heart disease. He knew from experience, a doctor wouldn't tell you any more than he wanted to.

"Is she recovering?" Neil asked.

"We can't answer you yet, Neil."

That's when he feared something even more threatening was taking place in his grandmother's frail body, in addition to her weak heartbeat and aftermath of a stroke.

Perhaps they were allowing visitors because she was failing fast.

Stella and Olivia came right after he called home. He wouldn't prevent this visit. His grandmother loved them, regardless of what deception had taken place. Hedda accompanied them. They came in quietly and stood near the door, staring at the quiet, still figure in the bed.

"It's my fault."

Neil could hardly believe who said that. "Hedda, how can you blame yourself for something like this?"

"I knew things," she said, "about Stella. We were arguing about it that day."

"No, it's my fault if anybody's," Stella said.

Olivia began to refute that, and so did Neil. They stopped suddenly when a moan sounded from the bed.

Neil went over and spoke to his grandmother, but she didn't respond. He looked at the women. "If we've hurt her, all we can do now is ask forgiveness. It's too late for blame and explanations."

"No it's not," came a feeble sound. Grandmother struggled to open her eyes but couldn't make it. "You just keep talking and talking, and I'm trying to get a good breath. That's what's killing me." She struggled. Her words were slurred. "I want to hear it all. Let's try again when I can sit up without my ribs hurting."

Neil had seen enough illness to know that sometimes a patient revived shortly before he or she died. He feared this was the case with his grandmother.

※

His grandmother seemed to feel better daily, but the doctors still claimed their tests and consultations were inconclusive. They wanted to keep her in the hospital until they were sure. Neil was a doctor—he knew that kind of talk was always bad news.

Finally, Grandmother was ready to hear everything. Neil, Olivia, Stella, and Hedda gathered outside her room. Neil went in while the others remained at the door.

His grandmother was propped up on pillows. "The doctors have their diagnosis," she said.

They hadn't told him. What was this? Neil opened his mouth to speak.

"No, Neil. I told them not to tell it until after I've talked to each of you." She gave an audible breath. "This still hurts, so don't make me talk too much. You're to do the talking."

Neil couldn't believe the doctors wouldn't have talked with him. Last year, they'd said she was dying. Why this secrecy now? "But. . .Grandmother—"

"Neil, I made them promise to not say anything yet. Before you hear it, I want the truth about what's being going on."

She motioned for the three women, still standing at the door, to sit on her bed.

Olivia and Hedda did. Stella held up a small bag. "I brought things to fix you up."

His grandmother nodded. Stella leaned over the bed and began to brush her hair. She held his grandmother's head out a little to get the back, then brushed and fluffed the waves around her face. Stella looked around. "Any of you can start at any time."

His grandmother let out a sound like a laugh turned into a yelp. "Eew, that hurt." She rolled her eyes up at Stella. "Don't make me laugh."

Hedda began. "We were arguing. She didn't want to hear it, but I kept on. To get away from me, she turned too quick and struck her hip on the corner of the kitchen table. Her cane slipped, and she fell across the table trying to catch herself. But she lost her balance and fell on the floor."

"Tell what we argued about, Hedda."

Hedda squeaked. "In front of them?"

"We're here to tell the truth, Hedda," Neil said. At least he hoped so. But how would he know the truth? Nothing was like he thought for the past ten months. Olivia was an actress, and he had no idea who or what Stella might be.

Hedda kept her head down. "It started the first day they came to the inn. I knew I'd seen Stella somewhere. Then I remembered. When me and Bart went down to Canaan Valley last year to visit our son and his wife, we went to the nickelodeon. Sure enough, there she was, playing the piano big as life."

That didn't surprise Neil. It sort of put some things in perspective. His grandmother's expression didn't change, and her eyes were closed.

"I felt it was my Christian duty to tell Mama McCory. The first time Stella played the piano at church, I told her I'd seen Stella play the piano in that nickelodeon. That it just wasn't right to come and sit on that piano bench in church and play the piano. I said that was being a hypocrite." She began to sob.

"Tell what I said about that, Hedda. It hurts my ribs to say too much."

"Yes, I'll tell it all." She took a handkerchief from her skirt pocket and made use of it. "Mama McCory said, 'Hedda sits in a nickelodeon while Stella plays the piano. Hedda sits in a church while Stella plays the piano. Now why is Stella a hypocrite and Hedda is not?' That's what she said." Her sobs were louder and her handkerchief wetter.

Stella turned and patted Hedda's shoulder. "I am a hypocrite."

"*We* are," Olivia said.

Stella nodded. "We're not good Christians. When we went to church, we pretended."

His grandmother held her ribs. "I told you not to do that." She turned her face toward Neil and gestured.

He would try. "I think what Grandmother means is that's what we all do in church. That's not bad, but it's what you do at home, at work, and in private that shows who you really are."

His grandmother nodded, so he must be doing all right. "But you don't do things to be a Christian. You do things because you are a Christian."

Stella's eyes got big. "So we weren't sinning?"

"Well. . .I. . .no. . .but. . .far as I know." He cleared his throat. "Basically, being a Christian is being a follower of Christ."

"Having Jesus in your heart?" Stella asked.

"Yes."

She shook her head. "Then we were sinning. We didn't get that done."

"Are you finished with me?" his grandmother asked.

"Oh. No." Stella finished her hair. "Now the truth about me. I'm a retired actress. And I'm not Olivia's mother; I'm her aunt—the sister of her father, Herman Easton."

"Hmm, I didn't know that part."

Neil wondered what "part" his grandmother did know.

Olivia spoke up. "My mother died when I was very young. Stella has been like a mother to me."

"Yes," his grandmother said, "I know the love you two have for each other. I saw it that first day, and it's never wavered. That isn't pretended."

"Now, I guess we get to the ad in the paper?" Stella asked.

Neil exhaled heavily. "That's where I come in."

His grandmother gave him a look. "I've known about that advertisement all along. Hedda showed it to me."

Hedda looked like she'd been wrung out. "She didn't want me to say anything. But things weren't right. I kept nagging about it. I kept saying the ladies weren't what they seemed to be." She wailed. "And all that time, I was being judgmental even though Mama McCory was so happy. I'm sorry. Please, everybody forgive me."

Everyone murmured his or her forgiveness.

"I don't understand, Grandmother. How could you know about the ad and not say anything?"

"Maybe we're cut from the same cloth, Neil." That look again. "At first I was shocked. Then I got to thinking. That gave me something to think about instead of lying in bed dying. I couldn't wait to see who in the world you'd bring home. I planned to expose you before you went through with any wedding."

"Why didn't you?"

She waited awhile before answering. Giving him a sidelong look and smiling, she finally said, "I liked Juliet. . .um, Olivia. If that delightful girl wanted the job of being my companion, I was all for it. I was ready to say, 'Let her have the job; you don't have to marry her.'"

Again, he asked, "Why didn't you?"

"When she served your cup of tea and you looked into her beautiful eyes, I felt like you were seeing a new world—one where Kathleen didn't live, one filled with possibilities. This girl was for you."

Was she? Olivia wasn't looking at anyone.

"At first I thought it would be wrong to marry for any reason but love. But I got to thinking further. In some countries the parents arrange the marriage. Why, right here in West Virginia, there was a time when mail-order brides came in. So I knew if you thought a girl would make me happy, that meant deep in your heart, even if you didn't know it, she would make you happy, too."

She patted Stella's hand. "Oh, and as for Stella, who wouldn't want this vivacious woman around? I felt like I'd found a new friend." They smiled fondly at each other. "There's something else you don't know."

Neil thought this was supposed to be their confession. It looked as if it was his grandmother's. "If you remember, when I looked at Stella, I said her eyes were unforgettable. Well, I knew exactly where I'd seen her, and it wasn't the nickelodeon. About fifteen years ago, a traveling troupe of actors came through here. Streun and I went to the performance. There was this beautiful young woman with long red hair and the greenest eyes imaginable, kicking up her heels and singing to beat the band. She made these mountains ring with music. When I remembered that, I realized who she was and thought that Olivia looked a lot like that young woman."

Neil could hardly believe what he was hearing, but Grandmother wasn't finished.

"Oh, I was already middle-aged when I saw her. But I thought if I was a young woman, I'd like to do that. I envied her. Then to have her in my house, being entertained by that famous actress every day has been such a joy."

She looked at Olivia. "And anyone would have to love this young lady."

"I didn't mean to do anything wrong," Olivia said.

Neil listened as she told of her dream to be an actress and said that her name was Olivia Easton. Her breath caught.

Stella interjected, "What's she's saying is that she's not legally married to Neil."

Neil felt it and knew it, but to hear it stated was like a knife in the heart.

"I came here for a job," Olivia said. "And from the beginning,

I wanted to be your companion. I didn't realize anyone would be hurt."

"I'm not hurt," his grandmother assured her. "I would have done anything to be an actress, too, if I was young like you. I think it's time this job with Neil ended."

He nodded, and his grandmother continued.

"If you want to stay on at the inn, I will hire you. If you want to go on to acting school, I would love to help out with that, too. I love you."

Neil had to leave the room. A man could take only so much of women hugging and crying all over each other.

Out walking the halls, he thought of his grandmother saying, *"And anyone would have to love this young lady."*

Neil didn't know about that. He didn't know Olivia Easton.

He'd fallen in love with an actress playing a part, not a real woman who returned his affection. How did one deal with being in love with a character in a play?

twenty-three

That afternoon Olivia said she was going for a walk and would be back soon. She hadn't really planned to go and see the pastor. It just seemed like the thing to do.

She didn't want Neil blamed at all but wanted Pastor Whitfield to know why she must leave Sunrise. She told him the entire story. "I'm sorry for pretending to be a fine Christian woman when I wasn't even sure what I believed."

"Olivia, I can't condone misrepresentation. But I can't condemn you either. If we place blame, we must also give credit. You've been good for Neil. He hasn't been this happy in years. You and Stella have brought laughter into people's lives. Mama McCory has lived longer than expected. The specialists said she would never be up and around again like she has been since you and Stella came."

"Stella says she and I can go back and live in her cabin if we need to. Do you think," she said, "if I confess to my father, who will probably disown me again, that I can clean up my life and be a good Christian?"

Olivia was shocked when he said, "No."

"Oh." She placed her hand on her heart.

Her feeling of devastation must have shown. He smiled kindly. "What I mean is that you don't need to wait until you clean up your life. First, just ask Jesus into your heart."

"I don't know how," she confessed.

"Just tell Him that you're sorry for your sins and ask Him to come into your heart."

"That's. . .all?"

"That's the first step. If you really mean it, then you'll want to live the way He tells us to live in the Bible. You pray and ask Him to show you how to live each day."

"I want to do that."

"Then pray after me."

She did. After they finished, she waited for a long time. Finally, she said, "I don't feel any different."

He smiled kindly. "It's not a magic potion. But you asked Jesus into your heart. He's there. You're a baby Christian right now."

"I think I understand," she said. "The Bible is my script. I need to read it and learn it and follow instructions on how to act on it."

"Exactly. And you'll find out that having Jesus in your heart isn't just a feeling. It's a knowing. You're now a part of God's family. And it's not just your heart; it's your life."

❧

When Neil walked into the church, he saw Olivia and the pastor standing at the front. She was wiping tears from her face.

He started to turn. "Come on in, Neil," the pastor said.

"I can come back later."

"No," Olivia said, "I was just leaving." When she passed him in the aisle, she said, "I told the pastor everything. I'm sorry." She hurried out.

Neil and the pastor both sat on the front row. Although Olivia had said she told him everything, Neil told his side of it.

"Neil, like I told Olivia, I'm not here to condone or condemn. I know good has come of this situation. But if you feel you've done wrong, you can always ask God's forgiveness. He's in that business, you know."

Neil gave a self-conscious laugh and nodded.

They prayed.

Afterward, the pastor said, "Olivia has given her life to Jesus."

Then she was a part of God's church, which Jesus called

"His bride." It was much more important for Olivia to be "the bride of Christ" than the bride of Dr. Neil McCory. Maybe some great good would come out of this situation. Perhaps God's plan for her life was for her to be a shining light in the acting world.

He could survive, although he didn't expect to ever love again. "Do I need to confess to the church?"

"Wait awhile," the pastor said. "Olivia said she may go to her father's. Who knows, she might decide to return and work at the inn. After all, the Lord works in mysterious ways."

Looking into the sympathetic eyes of the pastor, Neil knew he hadn't hidden his broken heart.

❧

Although it seemed all the truth was out now, including her having given her heart to the Lord, Olivia dreaded hearing the prognosis about Mama McCory. She and Stella sat on the bed and Neil in the chair when two doctors came in.

They were wearing long white smocks and carrying clipboards. "This has taken so long because we had to be sure. That's why all the tests, consultations, and waiting."

Olivia felt as stark as Neil and Stella looked. All the color seemed drained from them. Mama McCory looked fine, as if she could hold up under anything. Olivia admired her strength.

"It seems," the doctor said, "she's improving."

The moment of stunned silence was suddenly filled with their exclamations of joy and wonder and laughter.

Mama McCory smiled broadly. "I was afraid to say anything. Afraid it wouldn't be true. Oh, I knew I felt better after you two came, but anyone would. There was music, laughter, and love in the house again."

Olivia could only praise God. Yes, this must be what it felt like to have Jesus in one's heart.

They wept together. Even the doctors had moist eyes.

After the doctors left, Olivia said she was trying to be

truthful to everyone now. She needed to go and see her father. Knowing that she had to do it, she laid Mama McCory's locket in her hand.

"Remember, Olivia," she said, clasping the locket. "I'm your friend. And I know your heart is breaking. But whatever you decide to do, I'll be praying for you. Don't forget me."

"Oh, I could never do that."

She knew she could never forget Neil either. But there was no way she could stay at the inn. Mama McCory knew her heart ached for Neil. She would never be a good enough actress to hide that from him. She had to leave.

"I can't keep the money I made," she told Stella later as she was packing.

Stella nodded. "I know." Without either having to say it, she knew that Stella was aware she was in love with Neil. She left the money, rings, music box, and little black, jeweled handbag on the desk in Neil's study.

❧

Olivia didn't want to see Neil, so Stella took her to the depot. Neil must have felt the same way, because he hadn't been there for breakfast. Not until the train left Sunrise far behind did Olivia allow the tears to fall.

When Olivia arrived at her father's house, he and Evelyn greeted her warmly, although they gave her curious glances when she said Neil wasn't with her.

When they were settled in the parlor, Olivia said, "I need to talk."

Evelyn said softly, "I'll get us something to drink."

"No," Olivia said. "I can't let you be hospitable to me. This is not just a visit. You both need to hear what I have to say."

She told the whole story in the face of wide-eyed disbelief. She let none of that stop her. When she finished, her father stood and stared at her for a long time. He paced in front of her. She and Evelyn glanced at each other guardedly.

Finally, he turned and hit the palm of his hand with his fist.

"That took courage."

Courage? She'd be quaking in her boots if she hadn't been wearing her pointy-toed shoes.

He returned to a chair across from her. "I'm to blame, too, Olivia."

She couldn't believe it. He wasn't calling her a liar? Saying she was worse than a rogue and vagrant?

"I see now how much acting means to you. When I gave you an ultimatum, I thought you'd give in, give up the idea of being an actress. I thought I was protecting you."

He surprised her further by saying she was welcome to stay there as long as she wished. "Evelyn and I will go with you to New York and help you get settled there. You have our blessing."

Olivia should have been the happiest girl in the world, having come to know the Lord and now having her father's approval for an acting career. But she wasn't.

She thought and questioned for several days, then came to the conclusion that acting was not what she wanted after all. She wanted a real life, like managing an inn and having a husband and children.

She called Stella. First she asked about Mama McCory.

"She's improving every day," Stella said brightly. Then she told about going to the preacher and giving her own heart to Jesus. "Maybe we can be baptized together."

"Maybe someday," Olivia said. "But I've had a change in plans. Right now I don't feel like going to that acting school. I don't know what I'll do. For now, I need to study my Bible, attend church with Dad and Evelyn, and pray." She took a deep breath. "How is Neil?"

"Like all of us," Stella said, "he misses you."

"How do you know?"

"I'm smart."

They laughed, and Olivia said no more about it. Maybe Neil did miss her. She had done a good *job*.

&

Neil didn't feel as thankful this Thanksgiving as he had a year before.

"Holidays can be a sad time," Stella said when he sat heavily, thoughtfully, at the kitchen table and accepted a cup of coffee from her. She poured herself a cup and sat in front of him. "I heard from Olivia."

He stared at his cup. He wouldn't even act excited. She was probably in New York, living her dream.

"She's studying the Bible and has a good relationship with her father and Evelyn."

"That's good," Neil said blandly. He was glad about that, but self-pity seemed to take precedence. He'd had to reprimand himself for being glad people's illnesses kept him almost too busy to think. That didn't speak well for his own Christian life.

Suddenly Stella blurted out, "I have a confession."

Neil braced himself. What was it now? That he would lose this brightness in his life, too—along with Danny Quinn?

Stella sounded repentant as she told about the influence she had over Olivia. "I've basked in the admiration of Olivia—one of the few people, aside from actors, who thought I was in a respectable line of work."

Neil realized Stella wasn't acting but was being very honest and open with him. "I wanted to feel important in someone's eyes, and Olivia has been that someone to me."

"I know Olivia loves you very much."

Stella nodded. He saw the tears form in her eyes. "I believe, Neil, that part of her wanting to be an actress is her identifying with me. I have tried to take on a mother role for her, maybe selfishly because I never had a child. She needed someone after her mother died."

"Just so you know, Stella," Neil said. "I think now that Olivia has given her heart to the Lord, she could do a lot of good as a Christian actress." He scoffed. "I remember that she wouldn't even look at me that first day, and I came to the conclusion she was cross-eyed."

"You think of her often?"

Neil heard that intimation in her voice. He was tired of acting. "Yes, I do. Stella, she loved my grandmother. I really believed she was legally my wife, and in pretending, I sometimes forgot she wasn't."

"I think Olivia has had enough acting to last her for a lifetime. I've set her straight on a few things. The life of an actress has its disadvantages, too. I couldn't have done anything else. But I have suspected Olivia wanted to be like me more than she wanted to be an actress. She's reconsidering."

His head came up. "Reconsidering?"

"Yes. When a girl gets a taste of what a good husband can be like, it sort of takes precedence over a career."

"Is she. . .interested in someone?"

"Neil, I think that's for you to find out—since you are in love with her."

"But *she's* not in love with *me*." He looked at Stella for confirmation, but Stella simply looked at the ceiling and sighed as if she were bored to tears.

"I don't know if she cares for me that way," he added.

"You lived here with her for almost a year, Neil. You two liked each other. Do you think it was all an act?"

"I was trying to act like a dutiful, loving husband myself," he said. "Yet I condemned her for doing what I hired her to do." He gave an ironic laugh. "It's just that she did it better than I could have imagined."

"At least you can laugh about it now."

"That's all I can do," he said. "She gave back everything I gave to her. I can't just show up on her doorstep and expect her to greet me with open arms."

When she didn't answer, he asked, "Can I?"

Stella scoffed. "I should hope not. With an adventurous, imaginative girl like Olivia, that would seem so old-fashioned and dull."

twenty-four

Olivia got letters from Mama McCory at least once a week. She would tell what was going on with her, with the church, and with the inn. While reading her long, detailed letters, she could imagine all that Mama McCory described. Oh, how she would love to be there herself.

On Tuesday, Olivia called Stella. "You must come to Dad's for Christmas. You know you're welcome now. He's such a different person."

"I suppose we all are, Olivia," Stella said. "A lot will depend on the weather. You know how the snows are up here, and sometimes even the trains don't run. And you'll never believe this—Danny and I have talked seriously about getting married."

"You would leave the inn?"

"Oh, no. Danny and I both love it here. We'll stay as long as Mama McCory and Neil want us. And they say we're family and must never leave."

"I'm so glad for you, Stella. But. . .I thought you never wanted to marry again."

"Well, nobody does until the right one comes along. We girls make our plans, then *boom*! Some man comes along and changes them."

Olivia laughed lightly, but she felt a tug on her heartstrings. She knew exactly what Stella meant. "So, is Neil doing all right?"

"The usual, of course. He's busy at the hospital and clinic, and he still makes some house calls. With these telephones beginning to reach even up into the mountains, he's more in demand than ever."

"That's good, I guess. And I guess you're cooking the

breakfasts for the guests."

"Yes, and Danny helps since Hedda and Bart have officially retired. We have occasional, temporary help, but by the time a girl or woman gets trained, she leaves, like always. Neil is looking for help. There should be an ad in all the Sunday papers."

"What kind of help? A manager?"

"Oh dear. It's Bible study time, and here come the ladies. I'll talk to you later, dear. I love you."

"I love you, too," Olivia said almost absently. She did, of course, but she kept thinking how blessed Stella was to be at Sunrise Inn. Sometimes Olivia thought she was being punished because she had been deceptive to Mama McCory, all the people of Sunrise, and even Neil.

But Stella had been deceptive, too. She'd apparently been forgiven, for she surely was blessed now. She was living at the inn and had someone who wanted to marry her.

Olivia lectured herself often. She'd asked God to lead her into the kind of life that would be a blessing to others and would serve Him. Evelyn told her just to be patient and continue her Bible studies. God would let her know what He had for her when He was ready.

Olivia didn't find a lot of comfort in that. God might decide He wanted her to go somewhere far away from Sunrise Inn. . . and Neil.

After church on Sunday, she waited impatiently until her dad had finished with the newspaper, laid his head back in his chair, and closed his eyes while Evelyn sat before the fire with her needlepoint.

Olivia picked up the paper and whispered to Evelyn that she would be upstairs in her sitting room. Evelyn nodded sweetly and smiled. Although the thought made her even lonelier, Olivia was glad her dad had found a woman like Evelyn who complemented and perhaps even tamed him with her gentle nature.

As soon as she sat in the chair next to the window, Olivia

turned to the classifieds and searched the columns. Her mouth opened and she gasped. There it was, in much larger print than the other ads:

WANTED: A beautiful young woman with the initials J. K. or O. E. to marry an established man and live in a house large enough for a big family. Several months' experience necessary. Payment is love for a lifetime. If interested, please respond to DNMC, General Delivery, Post Office, Sunrise, West Virginia.

❧

On Monday, after making rounds at the hospital, Neil went to the post office, although he knew it was too soon for a response. He'd hoped Olivia would read the ad, think it clever, and respond.

By Tuesday, he felt like an idiot. On Wednesday, since Stella had errands to run in town, he asked her to check for a response. Stella stopped in and said there was no mail. "I could call her."

"No," Neil said. For the rest of the day he forced himself to concentrate on his patients. On the way home, he shivered in the cold and prayed for God to help him regain his joy. He'd accomplished what he'd set out to do, and that was to make his grandmother's last weeks and months happy ones. The Lord had allowed that. Not only had that made her happy, it had apparently given her an extended life, with no end in sight. Olivia had given his grandmother a new heart to live, but when she had left, she had taken his heart with her.

Danny came out to tend Sally when Neil arrived at the stable. Scrunching into his jacket and with head ducked to shield his face from the blustery cold wind, he made his way to the back door of the house, took off his gloves, and rubbed his hands together. He went into the kitchen where Stella was fixing supper. The aroma of baked bread and cake filled the room.

"Mama McCory and I thought we'd eat in the dining room tonight," she said. "Maybe that will cheer you up. Danny's having supper with us, and we want to talk to you about our business venture we've mentioned before. It should be ready by the time you're washed up."

Although he felt washed up already, Neil nodded. Winters and cold weather could be hard. Stella was lively and interesting, but it just wasn't the same without his "wife."

Having no secrets now, they'd shown his grandmother his "wanted" ad. She had said and kept saying, "The Lord will work out what's His will."

"The Lord can be awfully slow sometimes," Stella had quipped.

When he returned to the dining room, he thought the table looked especially nice, as if they were having company. The flickering candles emitted a comforting glow. He walked over to the fire and held out his hands, still feeling chilled.

"Um, Neil," he heard.

Without turning, he said, "Yes, Stella?"

"You didn't get a letter at the post office, but a young woman did come in by train. Her initials are J. O."

Neil felt his hands shake and told himself not to hope.

"Her name is Jenelle Owings."

Neil closed his eyes for a moment. No, he mustn't hope. That would be no stranger than some of the letters he'd gotten when he first put an ad in the paper. He took a deep breath, and slowly his head turned and he looked over his shoulder.

He felt like his eyes might pop out and he couldn't close his mouth. He couldn't even breathe. Standing between his grandmother and Stella was a pitiful-looking creature dressed in the most awful brown dress he'd ever seen—except once. Her hair was back in a tight bun, and she wore the most grotesque spectacles on her eyes that almost covered her entire face.

Stella's hand was over her mouth. Danny and Grandmother were chuckling. Neil took a few steps closer, and that's when he saw her crossed eyes behind those spectacles. He could only shake his head and try his best to give her a threatening look.

Before he could say anything, she whined, "Am I. . .beautiful enough?"

"To me, you're the most beautiful person in the world."

"Fine," Olivia said. "I'll stay this way."

"Will you now?" Neil spoke threateningly and walked closer. Her eyes uncrossed and widened. He reached up, took off the spectacles, and handed them to Stella.

Stella turned to Danny and Neil's grandmother. "I think we'd better get out of here."

They did, and Neil took Olivia in his arms, afraid to do more than brush his lips against her warm, soft ones. He then held her head close to his chest, feeling as if his heart might beat out of him. "I love you, Olivia."

"I love you, too, Dr. McCory," she said softly, and this time she looked very serious.

"I'll be back," he said.

Soon he returned with the others following. They all sat at the table and waited.

Neil came to her and fell to his knees. "Olivia," he said. "I have a proposal for you. I love you and I want you to be my wife."

"I accept." She looked as happy as he felt.

He took her hand and slipped his mother's engagement ring on her finger.

"Aren't you going to kiss her?" Danny said.

Neil rose. "I prefer to do that in private." He remembered the fake wedding in Stella's cabin. This time, however, he wouldn't just stand there and look over Olivia's head.

twenty-five

As if no one wanted any secrets anymore, they openly discussed wedding plans over the supper table.

"Do you want a big church wedding in Davidson?" Neil asked.

"I don't," Olivia said. "I would like a small ceremony at Sunrise Church, performed by Pastor Whitfield."

They all agreed that would be ideal. During the following days, Stella and Mama McCory would not tell Olivia or Neil what they were doing at church.

Olivia's dad and Evelyn came the day before the wedding to help. John and Sarah were unable to attend, as her baby was due in only a few weeks.

Finally, the big day arrived. The week before Christmas, Olivia stood in the doorway of the church. Neil walked to the front. Olivia's dad removed her coat from around her shoulders and laid it across a back pew.

The sanctuary was stunning. Red poinsettias were set all across the front. An arbor was set up in the center of the stage, decorated with greenery and white ribbons. A white rug lay on the floor in front of it.

Olivia felt breathless. All the people she loved so much were there, except for John and Sarah. The pastor, Neil, and Danny wore black suits, white shirts, and bow ties. Stella, standing as her matron of honor, looked beautiful in a green satin dress. Mama McCory wore a fur coat over her lace dress. She had returned the locket to Olivia as "something old." Evelyn, Bart, and Hedda sat next to Mama McCory on the front row.

Edith began to play "The Wedding March," and Olivia was in her white satin dress adorned with lace and seed pearls. She did not put the veil over her face but wanted to see her fiancée as she walked down the aisle, escorted by her dad.

She and Stella exchanged a sly glance when she handed her the bridal bouquet—a far cry from stinky marigolds. Evelyn said Herman had ordered the roses, and they'd come just in time. They looked beautiful against a background of green leaves and white baby's breath and tied with a white satin ribbon.

Olivia and Neil said their vows, the wedding band was slipped on her finger, and the preacher said, "I now pronounce you man and wife. You may kiss the bride."

Finally, the congratulations, hugs, and kisses ended. Her dad had rented a suite of rooms at the hotel for him, Evelyn, Stella, and Mama McCory. "I expect Stella and Mama here to show us what Sunrise is all about," her dad said. "I'd like to see the hospital and your clinic, Neil."

"We'll show him," Stella said.

"Expect us when you see us," Mama McCory said, waving at them as she left the church, seeming to be having the time of her life.

"I'm riding ahead of you two, and I'll take care of the horse and carriage," Danny said. "I'm staying with a buddy tonight. Your father's invited me to go with them tomorrow."

On the way to the inn, snow began to fall, as if showering a blanket of blessing on their wedding day. When the carriage pulled up in front of the inn, Olivia and Neil laughed. On a post, large as life, was a sign: No Room at the Inn.

They alighted from the carriage, and Danny appeared to take it out back. Olivia linked her arm through Neil's as they stood for a moment while the snow softly fell, turning the scenery into a winter wonderland.

Neil unlocked the door, then turned and brushed, not rice, but snow from her hair. His lips met hers for a moment. Cold as they were, they warmed her heart.

He swooped her up and set her inside the foyer, lighted

only by the lamp on the desk. Laughing, they removed their coats, hung them in the entry closet, and headed for the parlor to get warm.

The fire only needed to be stoked. He did that. She lit the candles on the Christmas tree, and the room danced with the firelight and glow from the tree.

She walked to the middle of the room, not quite certain what to do next. He came to her and looked up. She then looked. Overhead, hanging from the chandelier, was a ball of mistletoe.

With him standing so near and looking at her with eyes of love, she didn't need that as a cue to kiss her husband. Her arms encircled his neck as his hands came around her waist. She lifted her face to his. The musky fragrance was there as his head bent and his lips were a breath away.

She wanted no more pretenses. She preferred the reality of being in love and basking in the arms of her beloved who once had a bride idea.

A Letter To Our Readers

Dear Reader:

In order that we might better contribute to your reading enjoyment, we would appreciate your taking a few minutes to respond to the following questions. We welcome your comments and read each form and letter we receive. When completed, please return to the following:

Fiction Editor
Heartsong Presents
PO Box 719
Uhrichsville, Ohio 44683

1. Did you enjoy reading *A Bride Idea* by Yvonne Lehman?
   ❑ Very much! I would like to see more books by this author!
   ❑ Moderately. I would have enjoyed it more if

   _____

   _____

   _____

2. Are you a member of **Heartsong Presents**?   ❑ Yes   ❑ No
   If no, where did you purchase this book? _____

   _____

3. How would you rate, on a scale from 1 (poor) to 5 (superior), the cover design? _____

4. On a scale from 1 (poor) to 10 (superior), please rate the following elements.

   ____ Heroine   ____ Plot
   ____ Hero   ____ Inspirational theme
   ____ Setting   ____ Secondary characters

5. These characters were special because? _____

_____

_____

6. How has this book inspired your life? _____

_____

_____

7. What settings would you like to see covered in future **Heartsong Presents** books? _____

_____

_____

8. What are some inspirational themes you would like to see treated in future books? _____

_____

_____

9. Would you be interested in reading other **Heartsong Presents** titles? ❏ Yes ❏ No

10. Please check your age range:
   ❏ Under 18   ❏ 18-24
   ❏ 25-34   ❏ 35-45
   ❏ 46-55   ❏ Over 55

Name _____

Occupation _____

Address _____

City, State, Zip _____

KENTUCKY *Brides*

3 stories in 1

Three Kentucky women find that life isn't anything like they expected. Stories are by authors Lauralee Bliss, Irene B. Brand, and Yvonne Lehman.

Historical, paperback, 352 pages, 5³/₁₆" x 8"

_____

HEARTSONG
PRESENTS

If you love Christian romance…

$11.⁹⁹

You'll love Heartsong Presents' inspiring and faith-filled romances by today's very best Christian authors. . .Wanda E. Brunstetter, Mary Connealy, Susan Page Davis, Cathy Marie Hake, and Joyce Livingston, to mention a few!

When you join Heartsong Presents, you'll enjoy four brand-new, mass market, 176-page books—two contemporary and two historical—that will build you up in your faith when you discover God's role in every relationship you read about!

Mass Market 176 Pages

Imagine. . .four new romances every four weeks—with men and women like you who long to meet the one God has chosen as the love of their lives…all for the low price of $11.99 postpaid.

To join, simply visit www.heartsong presents.com or complete the coupon below and mail it to the address provided.

✂ -

YES! Sign me up for Hearts♥ng!

NEW MEMBERSHIPS WILL BE SHIPPED IMMEDIATELY!
Send no money now. We'll bill you only $11.99 postpaid with your first shipment of four books. Or for faster action, call 1-740-922-7280.

NAME _____

ADDRESS_____

CITY_____ STATE _____ ZIP _____

MAIL TO: HEARTSONG PRESENTS, P.O. Box 721, Uhrichsville, Ohio 44683
or sign up at **WWW.HEARTSONGPRESENTS.COM**